Mel Bay Presents

A NATURAL DEVELOPMENT IN DRUMMING TECHNIQUE

by Ronnie Ciago

CD CONTENTS

1	Match Grip Fulcrum Technique	[3:29]
2	Single Strike Roll	[0:37]
3	Double Strike Roll	[0:30]
4	5 Stroke Roll	[0:21]
5	9 Stroke Roll	[0:20]
6	Double Stroke Triplet Roll	[0:20]
7	7 Stroke Roll	[0:21]
8	13 Stroke Roll	[0:20]
9	Single Paradiddles - Ex. I	[0:23]
10	Single Paradiddles - Ex. II	[0:21]
11	Single Paradiddles - Ex. III	[0:20]
12	Single Paradiddles - Ex. IV	[0:20]
13	Single Paradiddles - Ex. V	[0:23]
14	Double Paradiddles - Ex. I	[0:21]
15	Double Paradiddles - Ex. II	[0:20]
16	Double Paradiddles - Ex. III	[0:20]
17	Double Paradiddles - Ex. IV	[0:20]
18	Double Paradiddles - Ex. V	[0:20]
19	Triple Paradiddles - Ex. I	[0:21]
20	Triple Paradiddles - Ex. II	[0:19]
21	Triple Paradiddles - Ex. III	[0:20]
22	Triple Paradiddles - Ex. IV	[0:20]
23	Triple Paradiddles - Ex. V	[0:20]
24	The Flam - Ex. I	[0:20]
25	The Flam - Ex. II	[0:20]
26	The Flam - Ex. II (A)	[0:17]
27	The Flam Tap - Ex.	[0:18]
28	The Flam Tap - Ex.	[0:14]
29	Swiss Army Triplets - Ex. I	[0:23]
30	Swiss Army Triplets - Ex. II	[0:21]
31	Swiss Army Triplets - Ex. III	[0:20]
32	Swiss Army Triplets - Ex. IV	[0:20]
33	Flam Paradiddles - Ex. I	[0:20]
34	Flam Paradiddles - Ex. II (A)	[0:19]
35	Flam Paradiddles - Ex. II (B)	[0:23]
36	Flam Paradiddles - Ex. II (A)	[0:24]
37	Flam Paradiddles - Ex. II (B)	[0:23]
38	The Drag - Ex. I	[0:17]
39	The Drag - Ex. II	[0:16]
40	Drag Paradiddles - Ex. I (Single Drag)	[0:17]
41	Drag Paradiddles - Ex. II A (Double Drag)	[0:22]
42	Drag Paradiddles - Ex. II B (Drag Double)	[0:23]
43	Drag Paradiddles - Ex. III A (Triple Drag)	[0:21]
44	Drag Paradiddles - Ex. III B (Drag Triple)	[0:23]
45	Three Stroke Ruff - Ex. I	[0:20]
46	Three Stroke Ruff Single Paradiddle - Ex. I	[0:22]
47	Three Stroke Ruff Double Paradiddle - Ex. II A	[0:25]
48	Three Stroke Ruff Double Paradiddle - Ex. II B	[0:22]
49	Three Stroke Ruff Triple Paradiddle - Ex. III A	[0:21]
50	Three Stroke Ruff Triple Paradiddle - Ex. III B	[0:23]
51	Four Stroke Ruff - Ex. I	[0:22]
52	Four Stroke Ruff Single Paradiddle - Ex. I	[0:21]
53	Four Stroke Ruff Double Paradiddle - Ex. II A	[0:21]
54	Four Stroke Ruff Double Paradiddle - Ex. II B	[0:20]
55	Four Stroke Ruff Triple Paradiddle - Ex. III A	[0:20]
56	Four Stroke Ruff Triple Paradiddle - Ex. III B	[0:20]
57	Paradiddle-diddles - Ex. I (A)	[0:20]
58	Paradiddle-diddles - Ex. I (B)	[0:20]
59	Paradiddle-diddles - Ex. II (A)	[0:19]
60	Paradiddle-diddles - Ex. II (B)	[0:19]
61	Single Ratamacue - Ex. I (A)	[0:17]
62	Single Ratamacue - Ex. I (B)	[0:19]
63	Double Ratamacue - Ex. II (A)	[0:21]
64	Double Ratamacue - Ex. II (B)	[0:22]
65	Triple Ratamacue - Ex. III (A)	[0:18]
66	Triple Ratamacue - Ex. III (B)	[0:15]

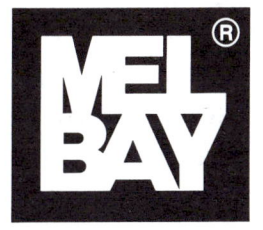

MEL BAY®

1 2 3 4 5 6 7 8 9 0

© 2004 BY MEL BAY PUBLICATIONS, INC., PACIFIC, MO 63069.
ALL RIGHTS RESERVED. INTERNATIONAL COPYRIGHT SECURED. B.M.I. MADE AND PRINTED IN U.S.A.
No part of this publication may be reproduced in whole or in part, or stored in a retrieval system, or transmitted in any form
or by any means, electronic, mechanical, photocopy, recording, or otherwise, without written permission of the publisher.

Visit us on the Web at www.melbay.com — E-mail us at email@melbay.com

ACKNOWLEDGMENTS

I'd like to thank the Mel Bay staff for putting it all together. I would also like to thank the following people and companies: Bill Ward, Patrick Moraz, Zoro, Kamen Percussion, Vic Firth, Paiste Cymbals, Evans Drum Heads, Brent Sorbom for his photos and my loving family Tai, Alecia and Angelo Ciago (Angelo has been playing drums since the age of 1 so look out).

Ronnie Ciago

ABOUT THE AUTHOR

Ronnie Ciago began playing drums at age 5. Growing up in New York he had the opportunity to study under Narada Michael Walden, Carmine Appice, Jim Chapin, Peter Haywood and Al Miller. Following high school, Ronnie moved to Boston to study at Berklee School of Music. At Berklee his studies included ear training, arranging, music theory, piano, and harmony. As a percussion major his drum teachers were Gary Chaffee and Kieth Copeland. After Berklee Ronnie began recording, touring, producing and teaching. He's recorded and toured with such artists as Bill Ward (Black Sabbath), Brand X, Mick Taylor (The Rolling Stones), Rickie Lee Jones, Riverdogs, Reeves Gabrels (David Bowie) and many others.

Congratulations on publishing A Natural Development in Drumming Technique. This book should prove to be a wonderful addition to the field of drum books concerning a very important subject - ambidexterity!

Kenwood Dennard

CONTENTS

I.	FOREWORD	4
II.	INTRODUCTION	5
III.	LEARNING AMBIDEXTERITY	8
	• Fulcrum Exercise	8
	• Practice Format	9
IV.	HAND DEVELOPMENT	10
	• Endurance Sticking Combinations	11
V.	DEVELOPING THE SINGLE STROKE ROLL—THE ACCENT	12
VI.	DEVELOPING THE DOUBLE STROKE OR EVEN ROLL	14
	• Five and Nine Stroke Rolls	15
	• Double Stroke (Triplet) Roll	16
	• Seven and Thirteen Stroke (Triplet) Rolls	17
VII.	PARADIDDLES	18
	• Single Paradiddles	18
	• Double Paradiddles	20
	• Triple Paradiddles	22
VIII.	THE FLAM • FLAM TAP	24
	• Swiss Army Triplets	26
	• Flam Paradiddles (single, double, triple)	28
IX.	THE DRAG	30
	• Drag Paradiddles (single, double, triple)	30
X.	THREE STROKE RUFF	32
	• Three Stroke Ruff Paradiddles (single, double, triple)	32
XI.	FOUR STROKE RUFF	34
	• Four Stroke Ruff Paradiddles (single, double, triple)	34
XII.	PARADIDDLE-DIDDLES	36
XIII.	RATAMACUES (single, double, triple)	37
XIV.	PHYSICAL ATTITUDE	39
XV.	MENTAL ATTITUDE	40

FOREWORD

This book was written for drummers with objective attitudes and for those who do not believe in having limitations in their technique. *A Natural Development in Drumming Technique* imparts the basic knowledge required to develop proficiency in the technique of ambidexterity. Therefore, each exercise herein will stress ambidexterity. So, whether your interests lie in jazz, rock, funk, Latin or classical drumming, this book will open up the other side of your playing!

INTRODUCTION

Rhythm is the organization of notes in time. It includes the elements of pulse, meter, tempo and metronomic accuracy. Rhythm gives life and form to music. The word rhythm is derived from the Greek word meaning "to flow." Musically, time must flow as rivers flow—not always at the same rate of speed, but always in motion. Rhythm coincides with all musical timing. A complete musical composition determines each of the following four items: how quickly the harmony changes, where the music will breathe, where the climax occurs, and how one section balances another in time.

As in music, life also has its rhythms. Blood flows through veins and arteries rhythmically. Thus, your pulse is similar to the pulsing of fundamental beats in a composition. In fact, most tempos are related to the average human pulse rate (i.e. (A NOTE SYMBOL) = 60, 90, 120, etc.). Also, people breathe in regular intervals (rhythmically) relative to how relaxed or excited they may be. **Ultimately, rhythm is a part of life!**

Think of rhythm in relationship to mathematics. Each note has its own value. Note values are based on numbers and fractions.

	Notes	Rests
whole	𝅝	𝄻
half	𝅗𝅥	𝄼
quarter	𝅘𝅥	𝄽
eigth	𝅘𝅥𝅮	𝄾
sixteenth	𝅘𝅥𝅯	𝄿
thirty-second	𝅘𝅥𝅰	𝅀
repeat mark		𝄇

In time signatures the top number indicates how many beats (pulses) are in each measure and the bottom number indicates the note value of each beat (pulse).

Standard Time Signatures											
2/4	3/4	4/4	5/4	6/4	7/4	3/8	5/8	6/8	7/8	9/8	11/8	12/8

Subdivision of beats in 4/4 time

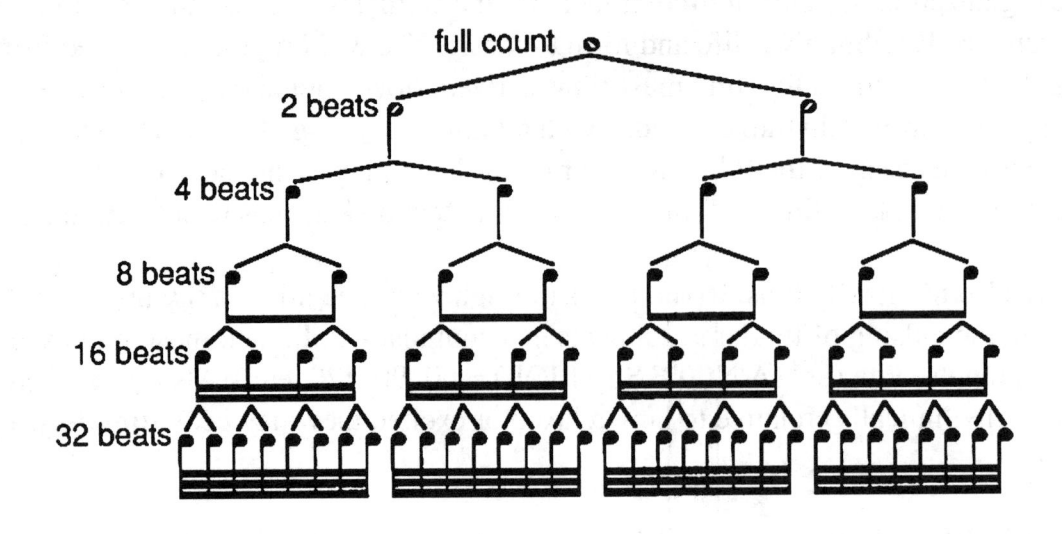

[Tree diagram showing rhythmic subdivisions:]
- full count (whole note)
- 2 beats (half notes)
- 4 beats (quarter notes)
- 8 beats (eighth notes)
- 16 beats (sixteenth notes)
- 32 beats (thirty-second notes)

A dot placed after any note (e.g., 𝅗𝅥.) increases the note's value by one half (e.g., 𝅗𝅥. = 𝅗𝅥 + ♩).

Match Grip Fulcrum Technique

• In the pictures **on the following page**, observe that the left and right hands appear to be mirror images of one another.

• The index finger is slightly bent with the stick lying in the crease of the first knuckle.

• The thumb is kept flat and parallel to the stick and adjacent to the index finger. Note the space between the thumb and index finger.

• The third, fourth and fifth fingers are cradling the stick loosely at the first crease of each finger in a relaxed natural posture with the butt end of the stick lying against the lower palm.

• When looking down at your sticks, the backs of your hands should be pointing upward. The stick should be in a line with the forearm.

• Keep your arms lowered and slightly above the pad or drum; this hand posture will prevent you from clinging to the sticks. Clinging to the sticks causes stiffness and tension which may prevent you from executing certain figures on the drums.

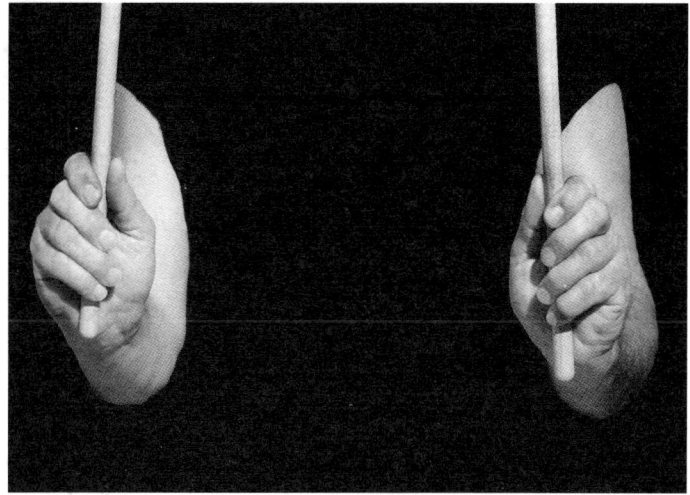

These two pictures show the proper *match grip fulcrum technique*.

Warming Up—Using the Metronome

Begin your warm ups with the *fulcrum exercise* of squeezing and releasing. This exercise focuses on strengthening the vital muscles in your hands, thus preventing the possibility of injury in the latter years of your drumming career. Statistics show most drummers using improper hand technique eventually do serious damage to their hands!

Warming up thirty minutes to an hour per day on a practice pad before playing your drum set will build up your speed, control and endurance. Begin each exercise with your metronome set at 60 beats per minute. As you feel relaxed with the lesson at this tempo...**stop!** Now, increase the tempo setting on the metronome. Eventually, you should be able to play at any tempo; however, don't become concerned with only playing for speed and continue the lesson at fast and slow tempos. This technique will develop your sense of time and give you an understanding of *placement value* relative to each note played. Think musically!

LEARNING AMBIDEXTERITY

Ambidexterity is the ability to use both hands with equal facility. These next exercises, done correctly, will encourage development in the right and left hemispheres of the brain (the right hemisphere controls the left hand and the left hemisphere controls the right hand).

Fulcrum Exercise

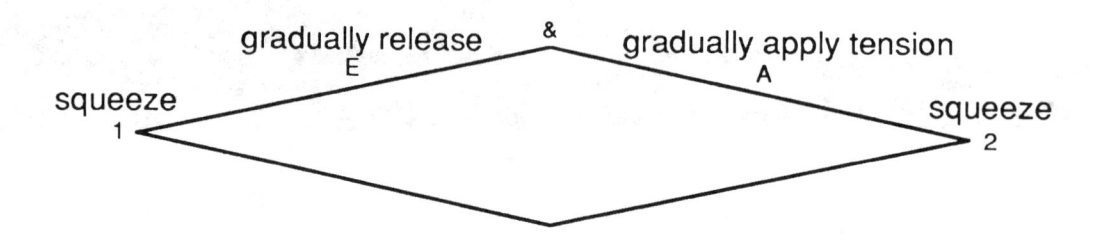

```
              gradually release    &    gradually apply tension
                      E                         A
squeeze                                                    squeeze
   1                                                          2
```

To execute this exercise properly, one must squeeze and release the stick, thus flexing the fulcrum (the muscle found between the thumb and index finger). You will be using the sixteenth note pulse in this exercise. The most tension is applied on the four downbeats. "E" and "&" are the release stages. "A" is where you begin applying pressure again. Squeeze and release four beats starting with your right hand. As you return to the count of "1" maintain pressure on the stick through four beats as the left hand repeats the exercise. Alternate hands through the exercise for fifteen minutes.

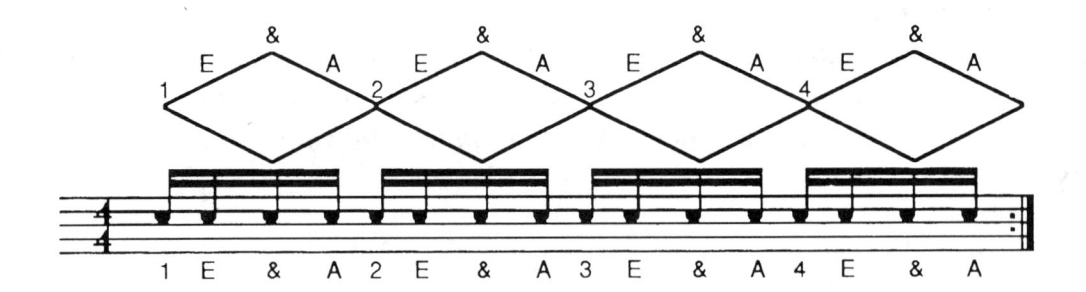

```
    &         &         &         &
 E    A    E    A    E    A    E    A
1    2    3    4
```

1 E & A 2 E & A 3 E & A 4 E & A

Set your metronome at 60 beats per minute. This will be the stationary metronome exercise. Practice slowly and precisely while focusing on the muscle which you are working out. **Remember, never increase the metronome speed during this exercise and always alternate hands at the repeat mark!**

Practice Format

• Using the *match grip fulcrum technique*, practice exercises (1-4) squeezing and releasing quarter notes. Maintain pressure on the stick at the last beat of each measure (before the sticking change) as the opposite hand continues the exercise. Place the inactive sticks on the pad. **Do not strike the pad with the stick at this time!**

• Now, squeeze and release quarters while squeezing and releasing eighths on the opposite hand. **Again, do not strike the sticks on the pad.**

• Now, playing only quarters strike the practice pad with a downward wrist action. **Use the wrist only!**

• Now, play quarters, and squeeze and release eighths with the opposite hand (held at a 45 degree angle).

• Practice this routine thirty minutes every day as a prelude to your warm-up exercises.

Opposite Hand Sticking

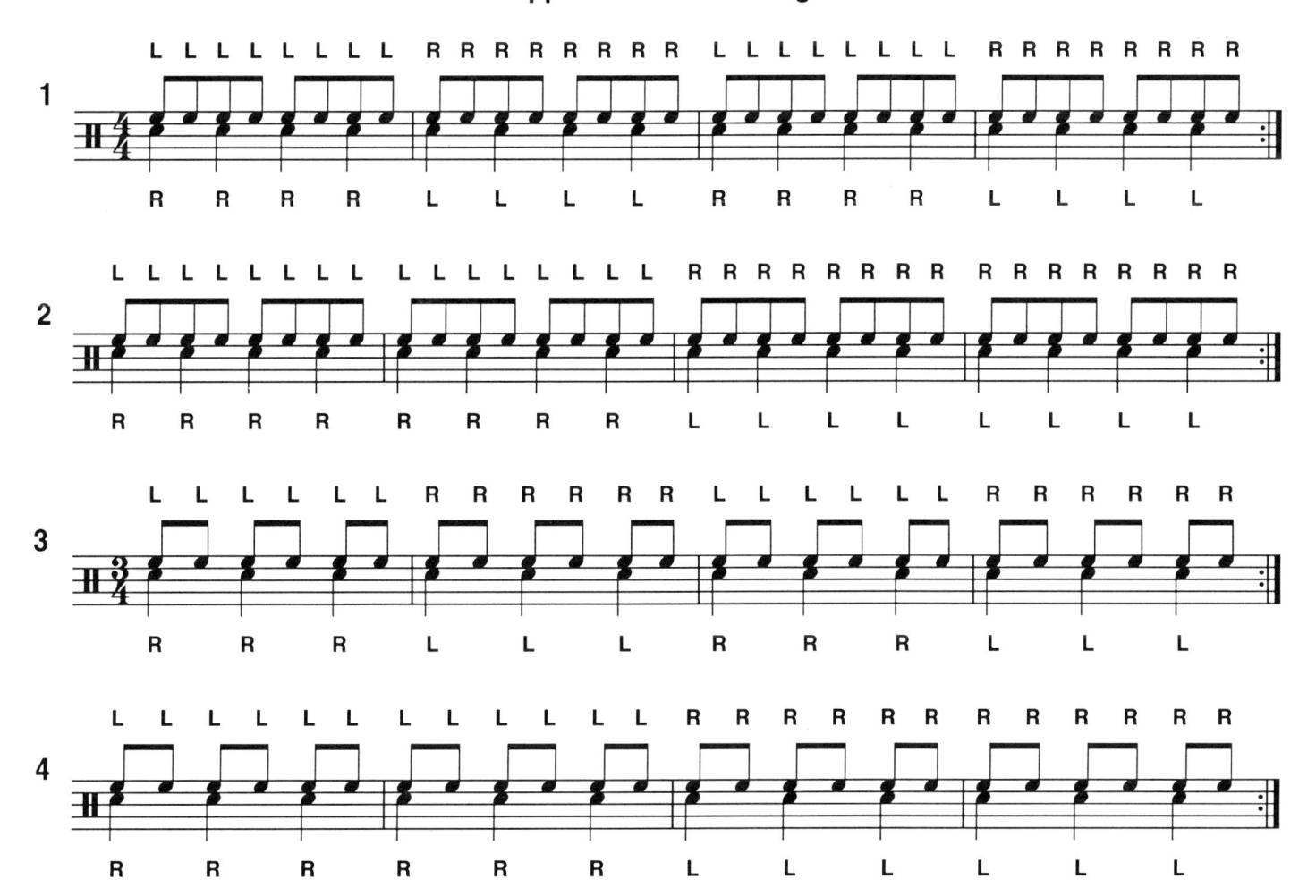

1.
Top: L L L L L L L L R R R R R R R R L L L L L L L L R R R R R R R R
Bottom: R R R R L L L L R R R R L L L L

2.
Top: L L L L L L L L L L L L L L L L R R R R R R R R R R R R R R R R
Bottom: R R R R R R R R L L L L L L L L

3. (3/4)
Top: L L L L L L R R R R R R L L L L L L R R R R R R
Bottom: R R R L L L R R R L L L

4.
Top: L L L L L L L L L L L L R R R R R R R R R R R R
Bottom: R R R R R R L L L L L L

HAND DEVELOPMENT

The following exercises are played in a drumming context (i.e. striking the drum with the stick). In this case, use your practice pad for the warm-up figures. Use the same metronome format described in the introduction. With proper practice technique, the exercises you are about to undertake will enable you to acquire preciseness of execution, control, speed, endurance, flexibility and development of your time accuracy. These seven techniques are used for your hand development: 1) fulcrum 2) wrist 3) finger 4) & 5) match and traditional hand positions (incorporated in your practice procedure) and 6) & 7) use of right and left hand leads (throughout the book to assure equal time is put into both hands). These exercises must be practiced regularly and intelligently using full focus and concentration. Always keep in mind the fact that there should be no limitations to your drumming technique!

Begin practicing the endurance sticking combinations (please, see the exercises on the next page) at a slow tempo. As you begin to feel more relaxed, gradually increase the speed. Note, these exercises begin with right hand leads, but change to left hand leads at the repeat, thus creating cyclic sticking combinations. Also, note that your foot is on quarter notes.

Endurance Sticking Combinations

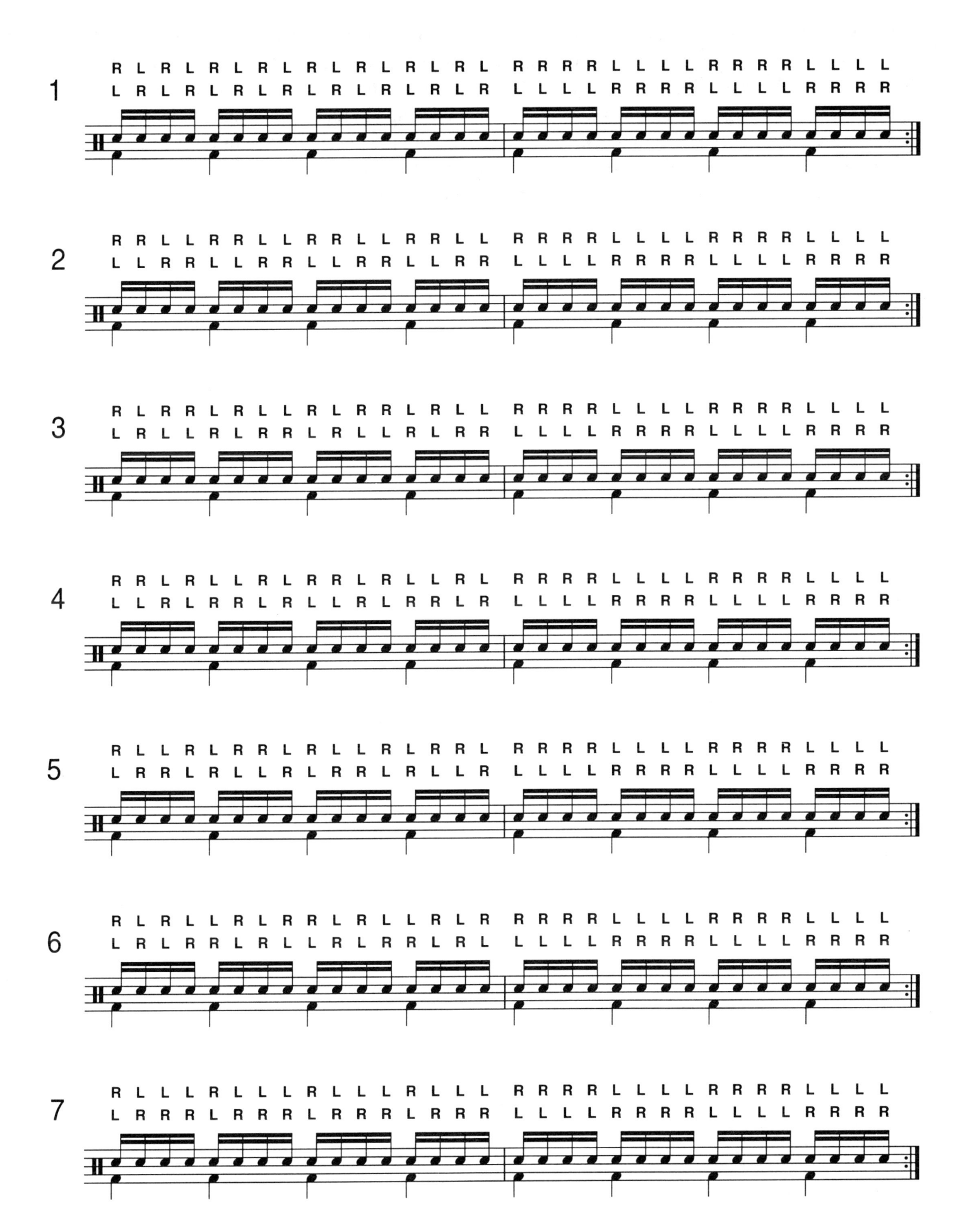

1
R L R L R L R L R L R L R L R L   R R R R L L L L R R R R L L L L
L R L R L R L R L R L R L R L R   L L L L R R R R L L L L R R R R

2
R R L L R R L L R R L L R R L L   R R R R L L L L R R R R L L L L
L L R R L L R R L L R R L L R R   L L L L R R R R L L L L R R R R

3
R L R R L R L L R L R R L R L L   R R R R L L L L R R R R L L L L
L R L L R L R R L R L L R L R R   L L L L R R R R L L L L R R R R

4
R R L R L L R L R R L R L L R L   R R R R L L L L R R R R L L L L
L L R L R R L R L L R L R R L R   L L L L R R R R L L L L R R R R

5
R L L R L R R L R L L R L R R L   R R R R L L L L R R R R L L L L
L R R L R L L R L R R L R L L R   L L L L R R R R L L L L R R R R

6
R L R L L R L R L R L L R L R L   R R R R L L L L R R R R L L L L
L R L R R L R L R L R R L R L R   L L L L R R R R L L L L R R R R

7
R L L L R L L L R L L L R L L L   R R R R L L L L R R R R L L L L
L R R R L R R R L R R R L R R R   L L L L R R R R L L L L R R R R

DEVELOPING THE SINGLE STROKE ROLL—THE ACCENT

The single stroke roll is executed with alternate single strokes. Begin with the metronome set to 60 beats per minute. (As you become comfortable with this exercise, you will be able to increase the tempo, yet retain your ability to play evenly.) The accent (>) is an indication of special emphasis on the given note. This designates that the accented note should sound louder than those without accent symbols. The accent is executed by a quick pop or squeeze from the fulcrum. As your proficiency with the single stroke roll increases, you will omit the accent (as the accent is used merely as a point of reference of time), yet continue to play the roll evenly. Please, see the exercises on the next page.

Single Stroke Roll—The Accent

DEVELOPING THE DOUBLE STROKE OR EVEN ROLL

Begin playing the roll at a slow tempo (i.e. 60 beats per minute). This is an alternate playing of two strokes with each hand where each stroke is played with an equal amount of volume and control. The quarter and eighth notes will be played with just the wrists. As you increase your speed or note values to 16th and 32nd notes the first stroke is executed normally and the second stroke is bounced. The fingers will control the bounce. As your roll speed increases you must focus on relaxing the muscles of your wrists, hands and arms. **Remember, keep every stroke perfectly even and utilize right and left hand leads.**

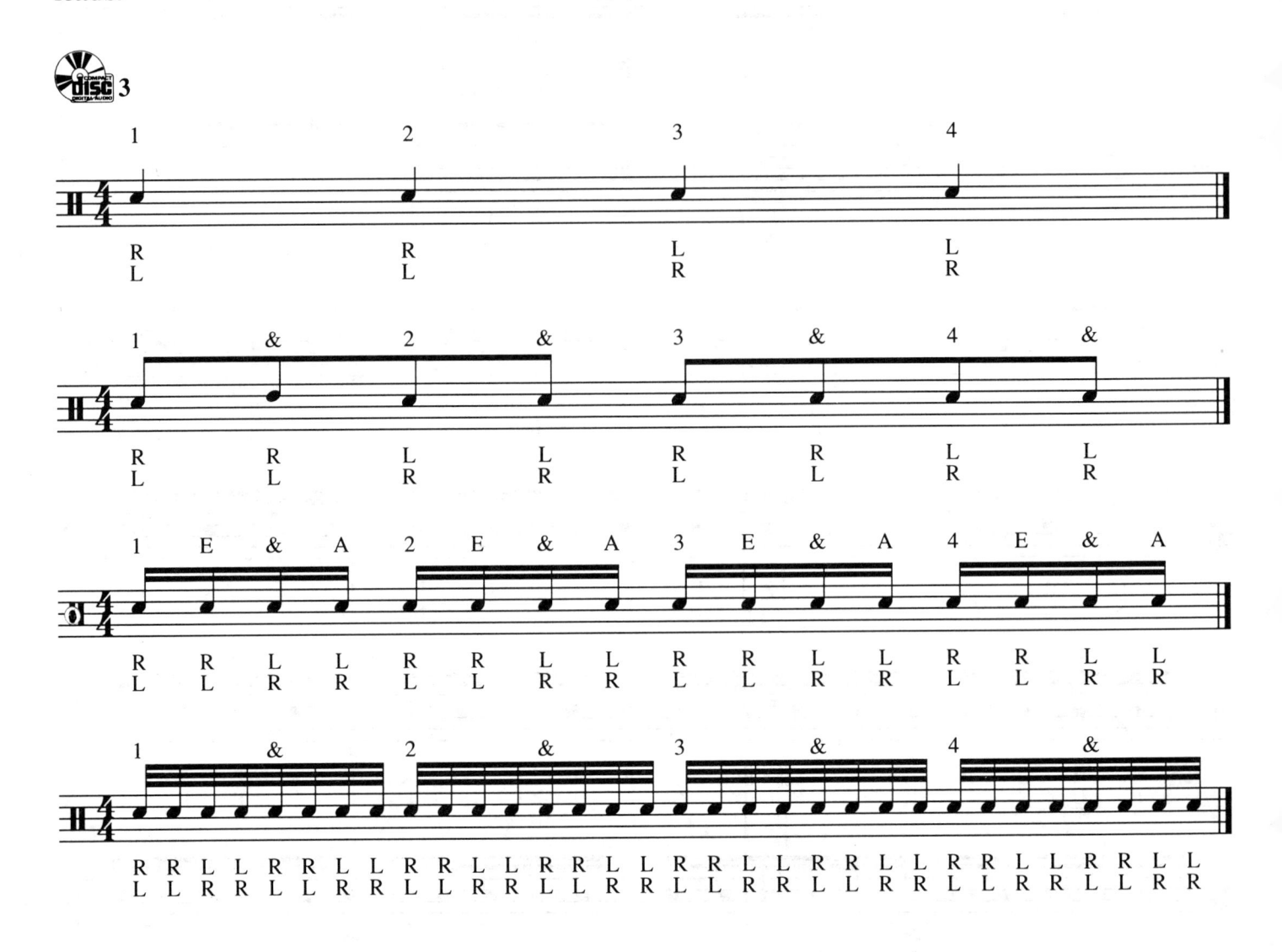

5 and 9 Stroke Rolls

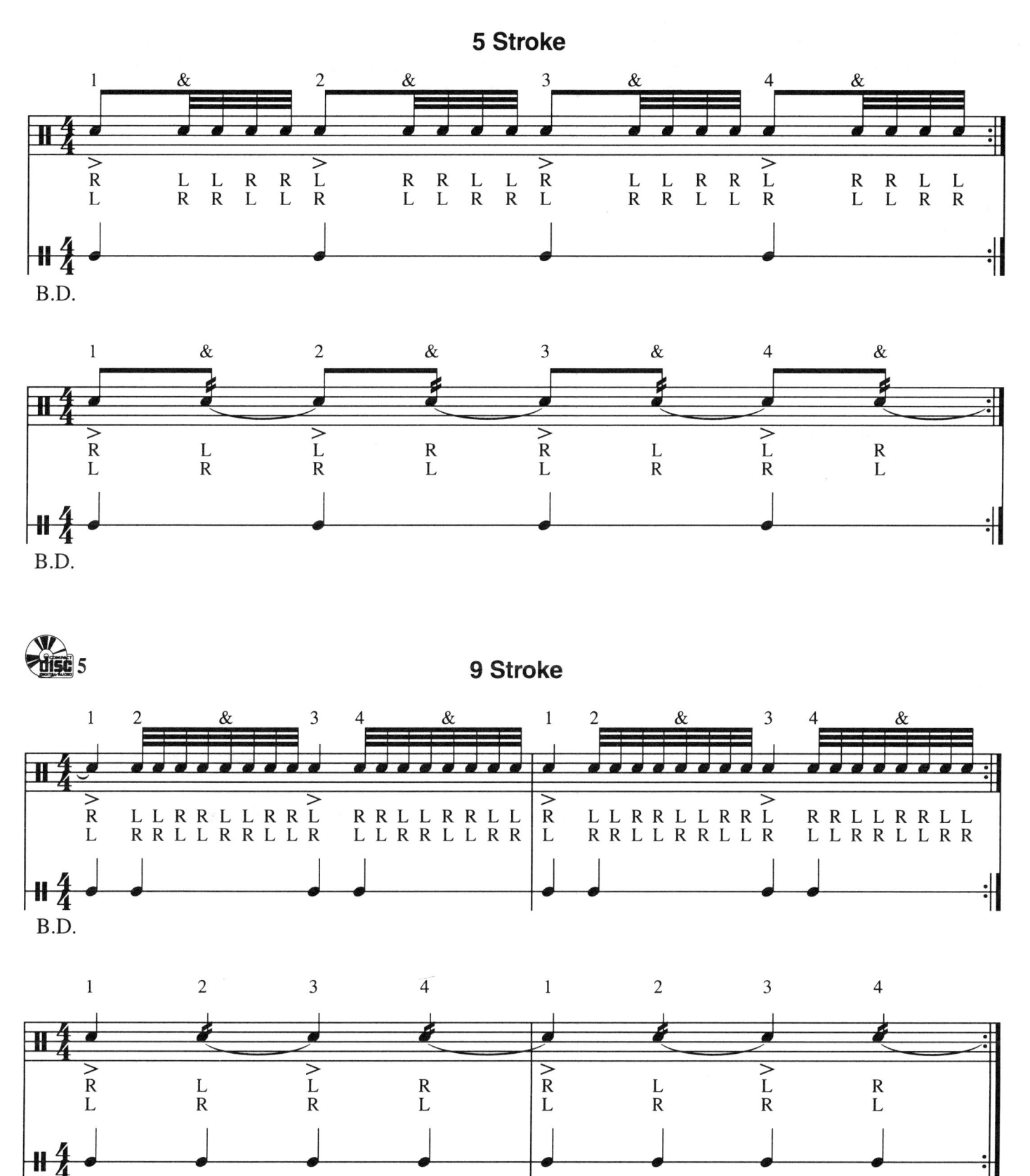

5 Stroke

Execute rolls with and without accents!

Double-Stroke (Triplet) Roll

In the execution of this rudiment the double strokes are in triplet form. Practice slowly and precisely utilizing the triplet pulse. As you become familiar with this rudiment, increase the speed. Be certain each stroke is executed with an equal amount of volume and control.

Example I

To execute the press roll or crush roll you must press each double stroke against the head of the drum.

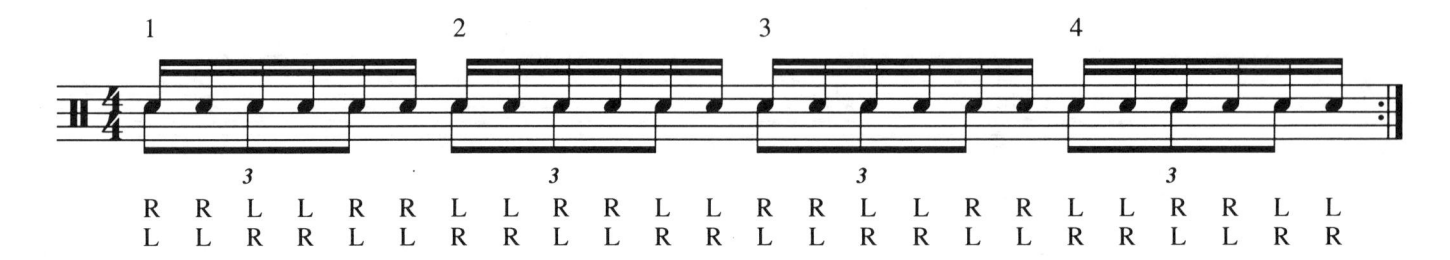

```
1                 2                 3                 4
R R L L R R L L   R R L L R R L L   R R L L R R L L   R R L L R R L L
L L R R L L R R   L L R R L L R R   L L R R L L R R   L L R R L L R R
```

Example II

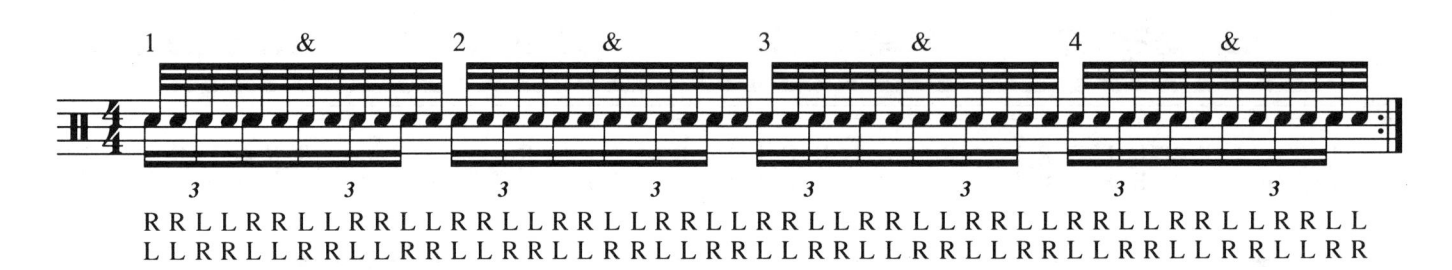

```
1     &     2     &     3     &     4     &
R R L L R R L L R R L L R R L L R R L L R R L L R R L L R R L L
L L R R L L R R L L R R L L R R L L R R L L R R L L R R L L R R
```

Note: You must be able to discern the difference between even and triplet rolls. The number of strokes in the roll will determine whether it is even or triplet.

7 and 13 Stroke (Triplet) Rolls

7 Stroke

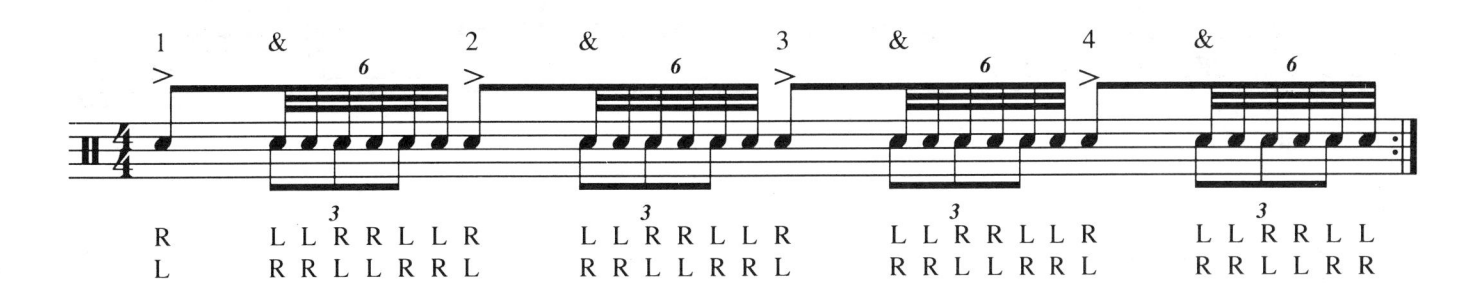

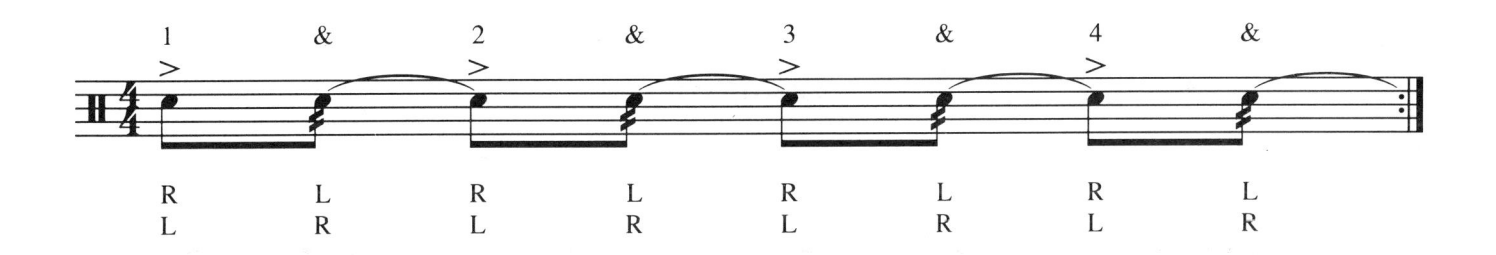

1 & 6 2 & 6 3 & 6 4 & 6

R LLRRLLR   LLRRLLR   LLRRLLR   LLRRLL
L RRLLRRL   RRLLRRL   RRLLRRL   RRLLRR

1 & 2 & 3 & 4 &

R L R L R L R L
L R L R L R L R

13 Stroke

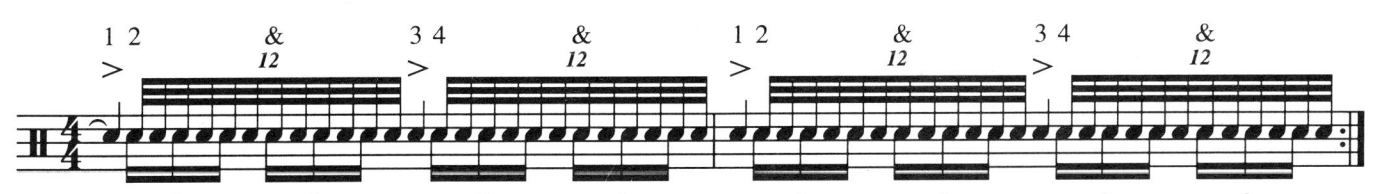

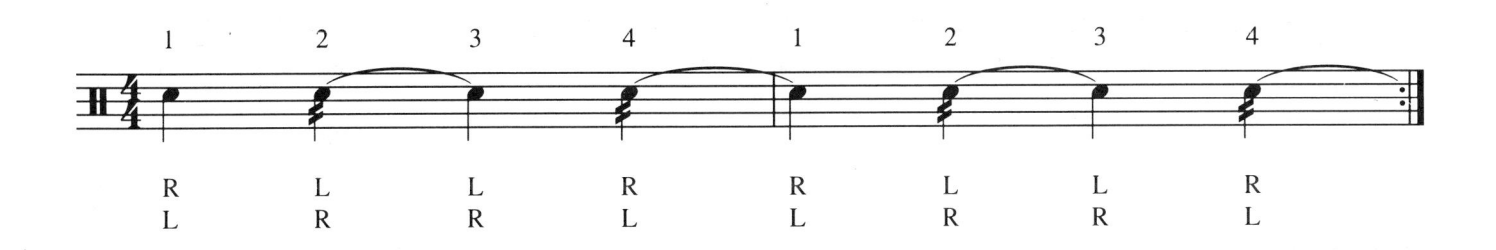

1 2 & 12 3 4 & 12 1 2 & 12 3 4 & 12

RLLRRLLRRLLRR LRRLLRRLLRRLL RLLRRLLRRLLRR LRRLLRRLLRRLL
LRRLLRRLLRRLL RLLRRLLRRLLRR LRRLLRRLLRRLL RLLRRLLRRLLRR

1 2 3 4 1 2 3 4

R L L R R L L R
L R R L L R R L

17

Single Paradiddles

Example I

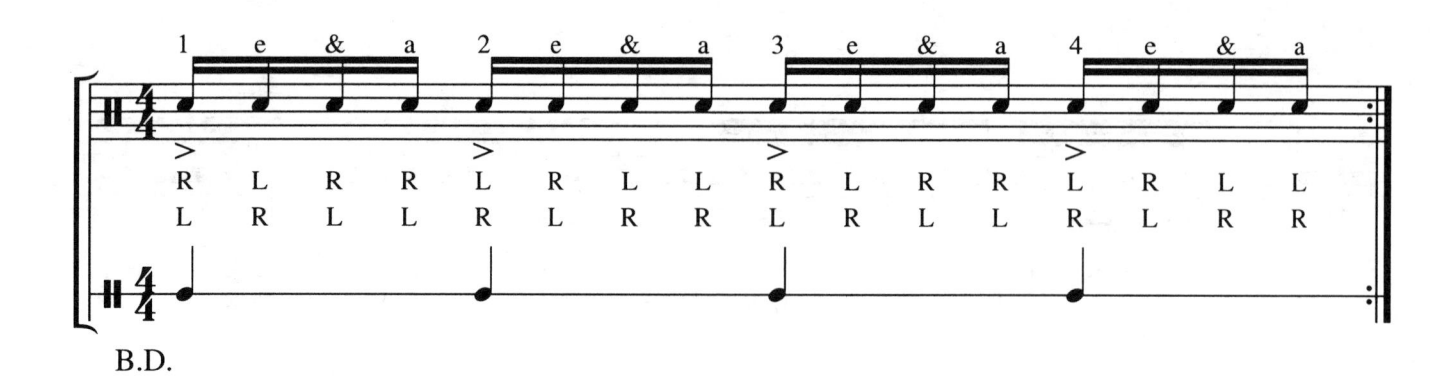

1	e	&	a	2	e	&	a	3	e	&	a	4	e	&	a
>R	L	R	R	>L	R	L	L	>R	L	R	R	>L	R	L	L
L	R	L	L	R	L	R	R	L	R	L	L	R	L	R	R

B.D.

Example II

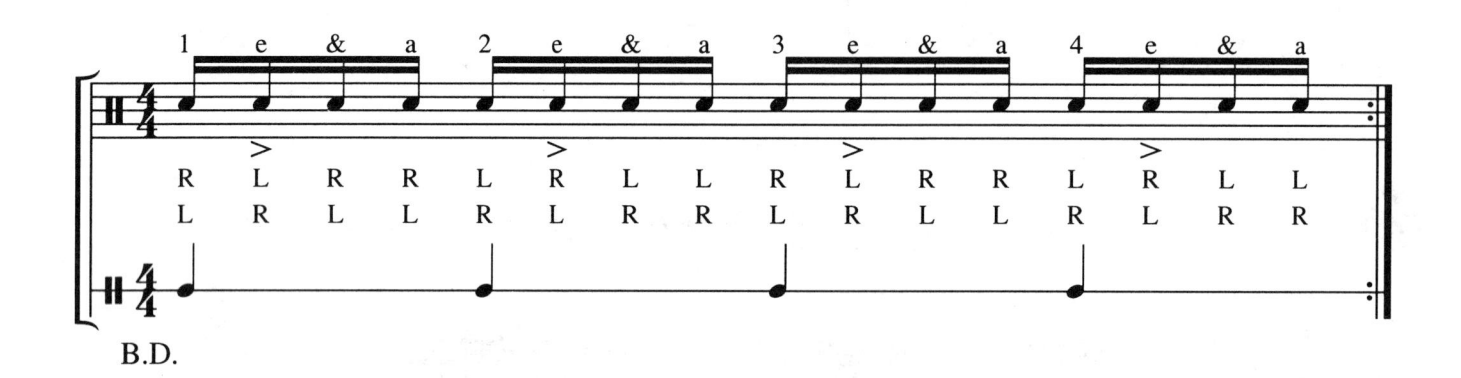

1	e	&	a	2	e	&	a	3	e	&	a	4	e	&	a
R	>L	R	R	L	>R	L	L	R	>L	R	R	L	>R	L	L
L	R	L	L	R	L	R	R	L	R	L	L	R	L	R	R

B.D.

Example III

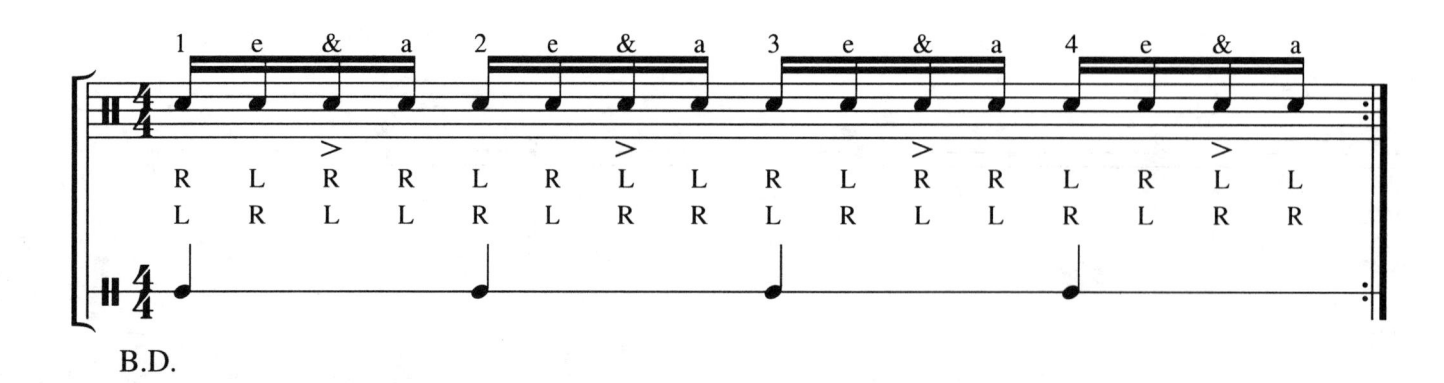

1	e	&	a	2	e	&	a	3	e	&	a	4	e	&	a
R	L	>R	R	L	R	>L	L	R	L	>R	R	L	R	>L	L
L	R	L	L	R	L	R	R	L	R	L	L	R	L	R	R

B.D.

Example IV

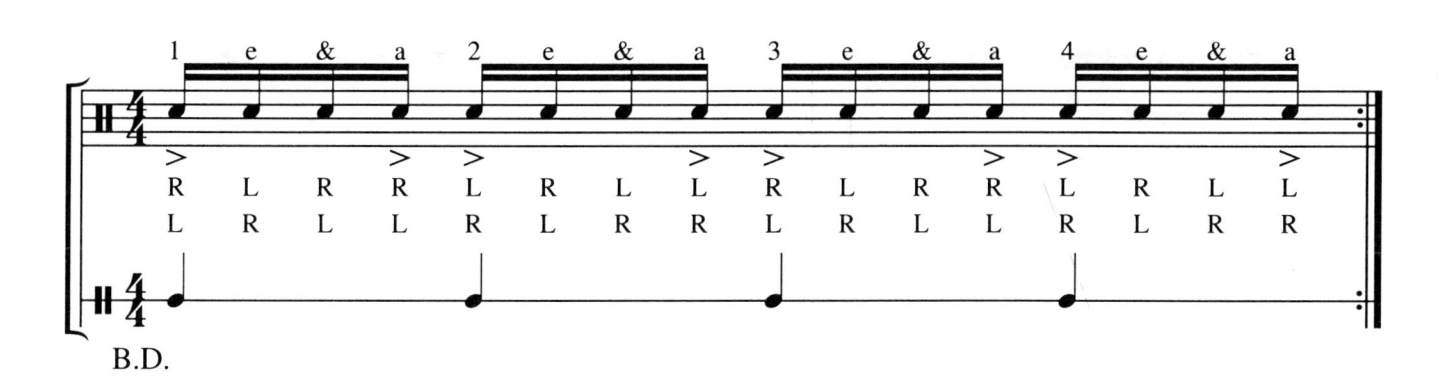

	1	e	&	a	2	e	&	a	3	e	&	a	4	e	&	a
Accent	>				>	>			>	>			>			>
Top	R	L	R	R	L	R	L	L	R	L	R	R	L	R	L	L
Bottom	L	R	L	L	R	L	R	R	L	R	L	L	R	L	R	R

B.D. on each quarter note.

Example V

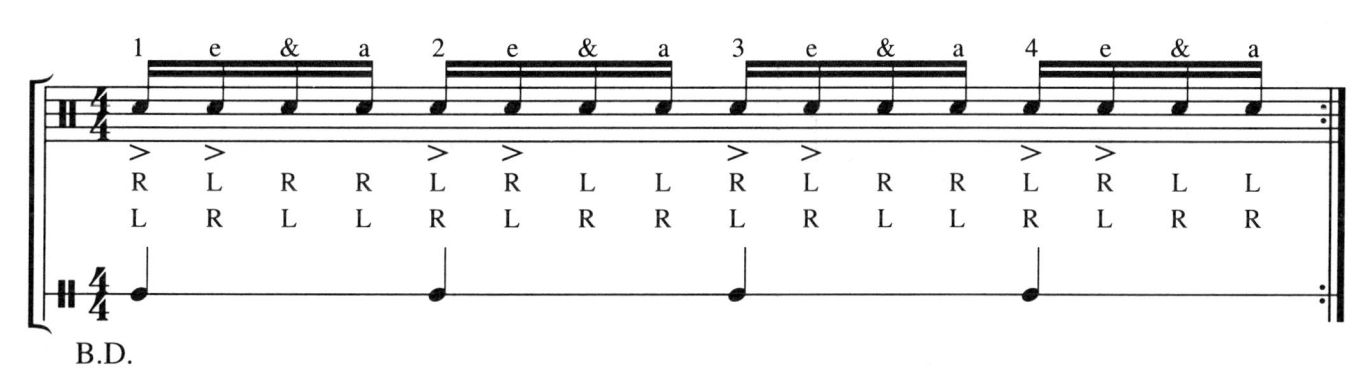

	1	e	&	a	2	e	&	a	3	e	&	a	4	e	&	a
Accent	>	>			>	>			>	>			>	>		
Top	R	L	R	R	L	R	L	L	R	L	R	R	L	R	L	L
Bottom	L	R	L	L	R	L	R	R	L	R	L	L	R	L	R	R

B.D. on each quarter note.

Double Paradiddles

Example I

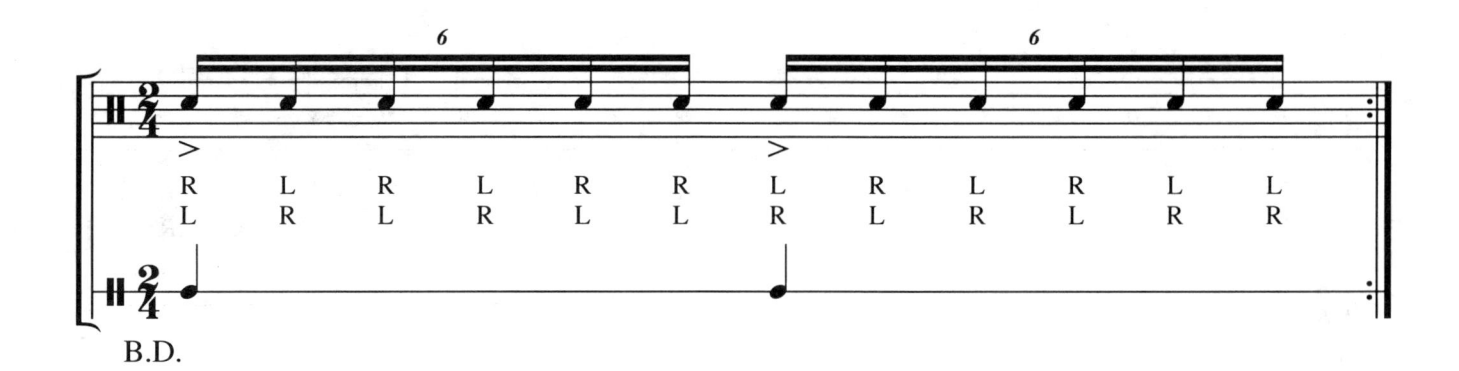

Example II

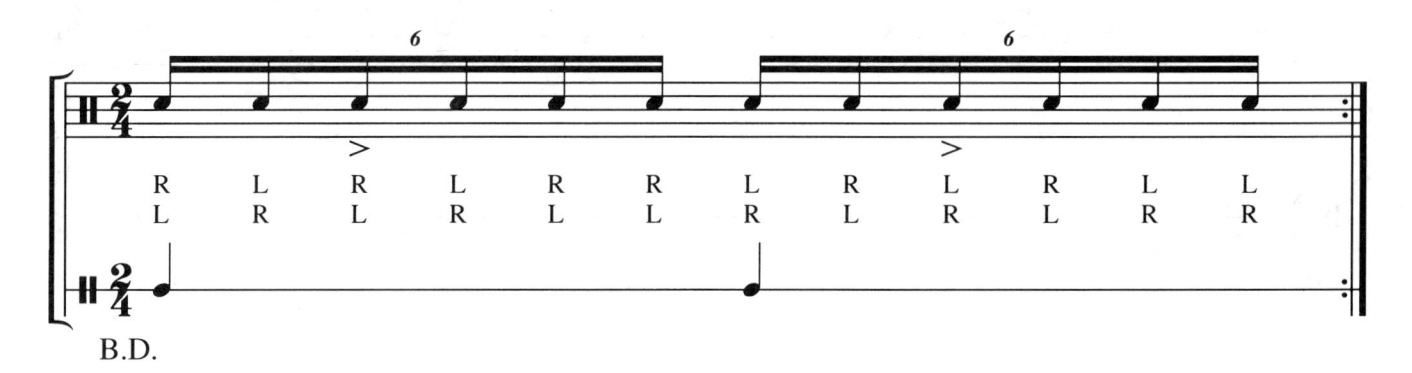

Example III

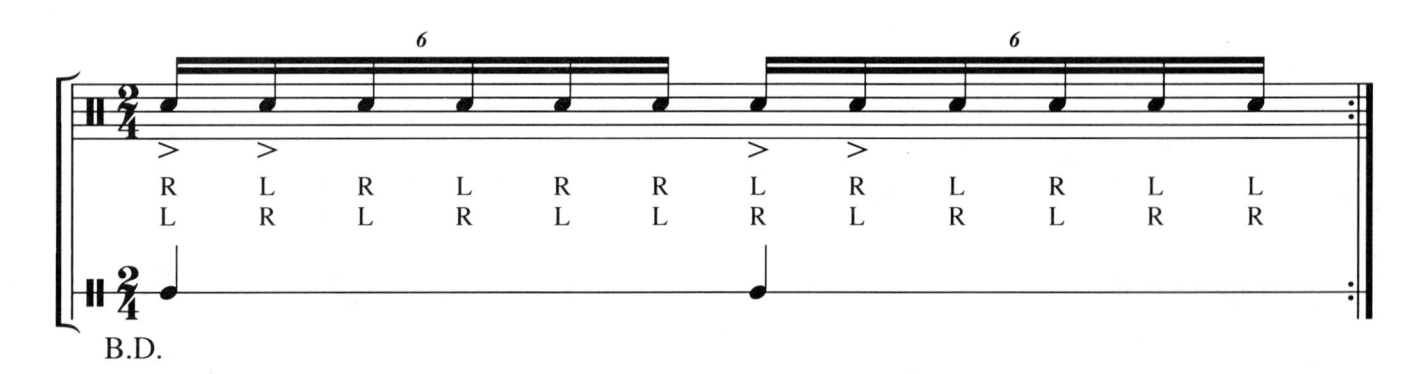

20

Example IV

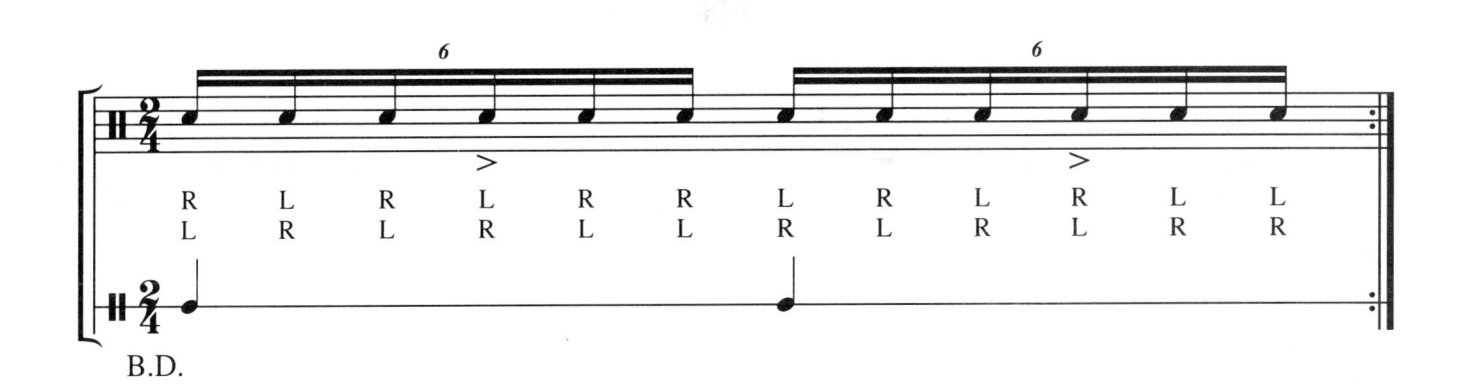

(CD 17)

Example V

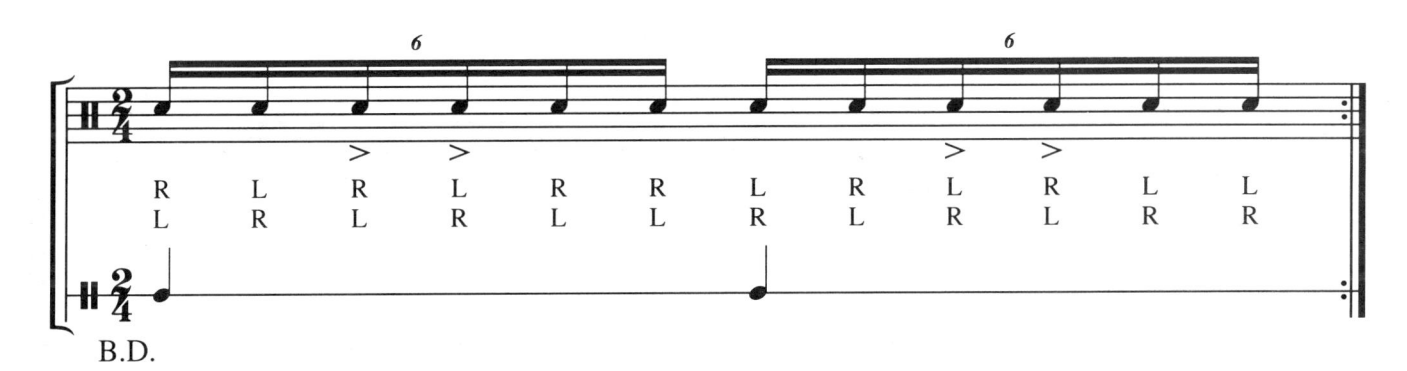

(CD 18)

Triple Paradiddles

Example I

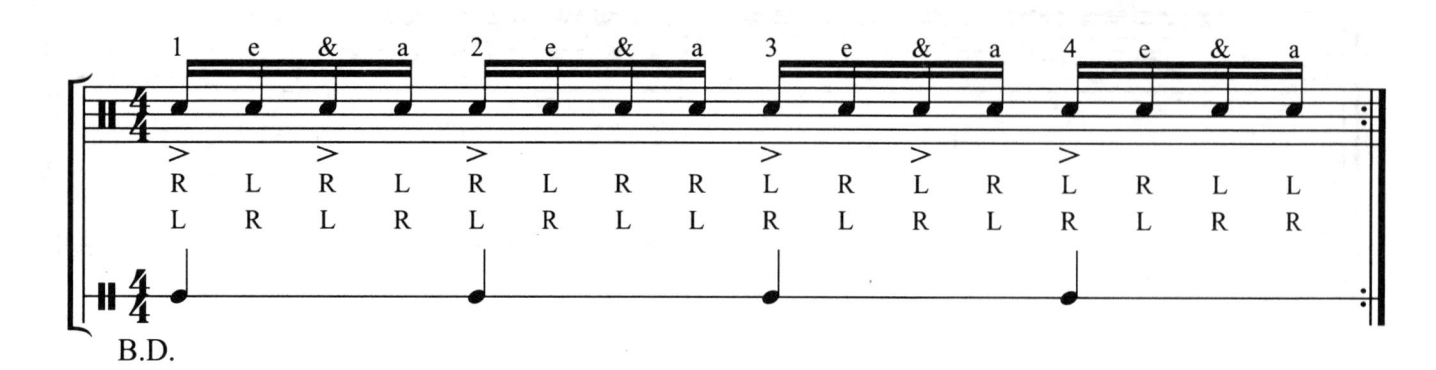

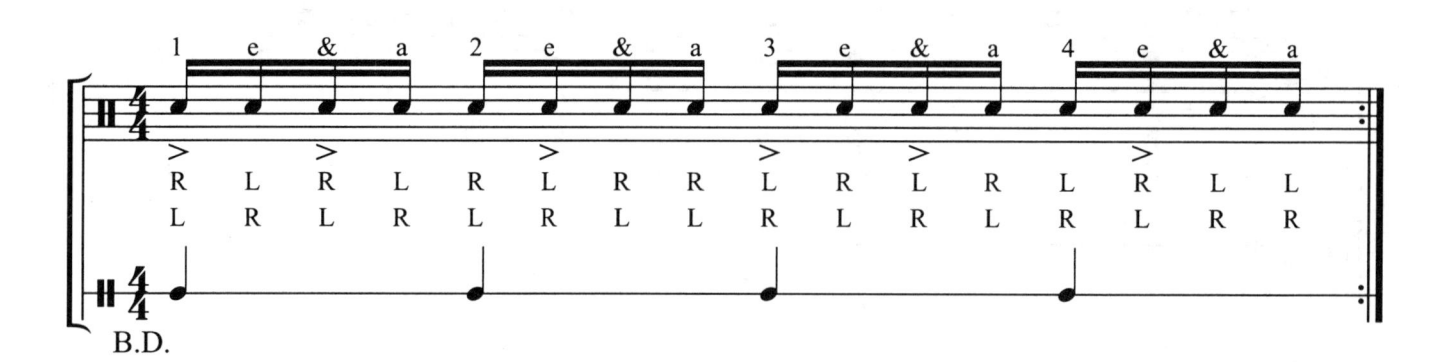

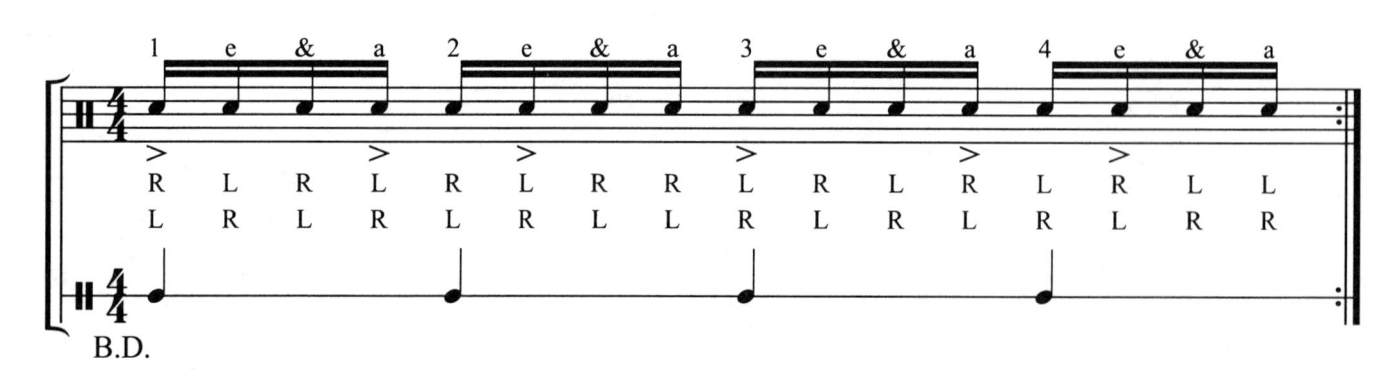

Example IV

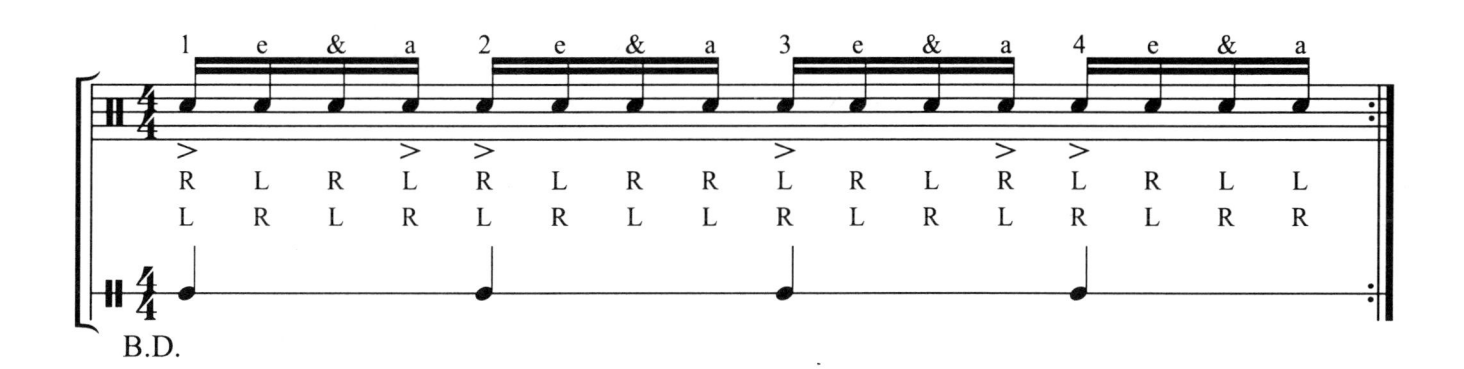

(CD 22)

Example V

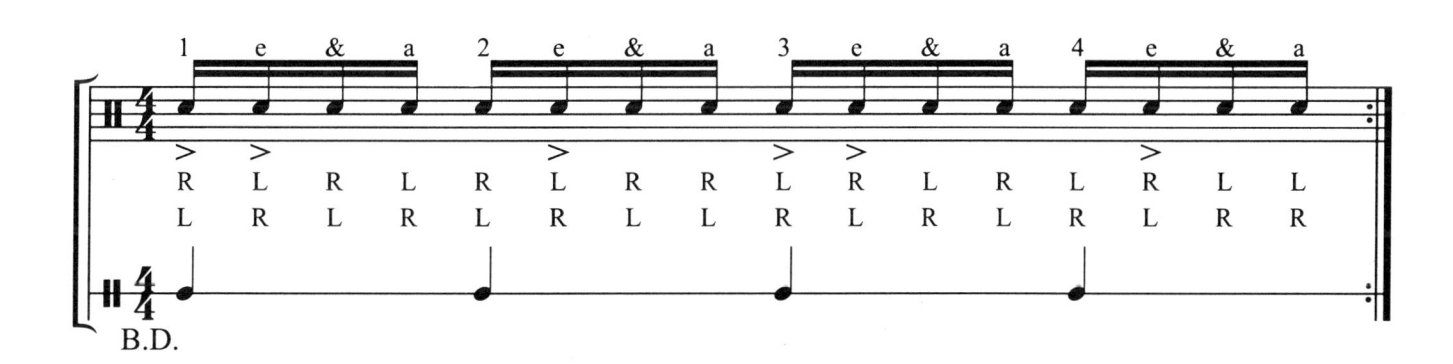

(CD 23)

THE FLAM

The *flam* is executed by playing a *grace note* with a *primary note* immediately following. The grace note is played lightly and very close to the primary note making it sound as if only one note is being played.

F = right hand flam   Ⓕ = left hand flam

Example I

Example II

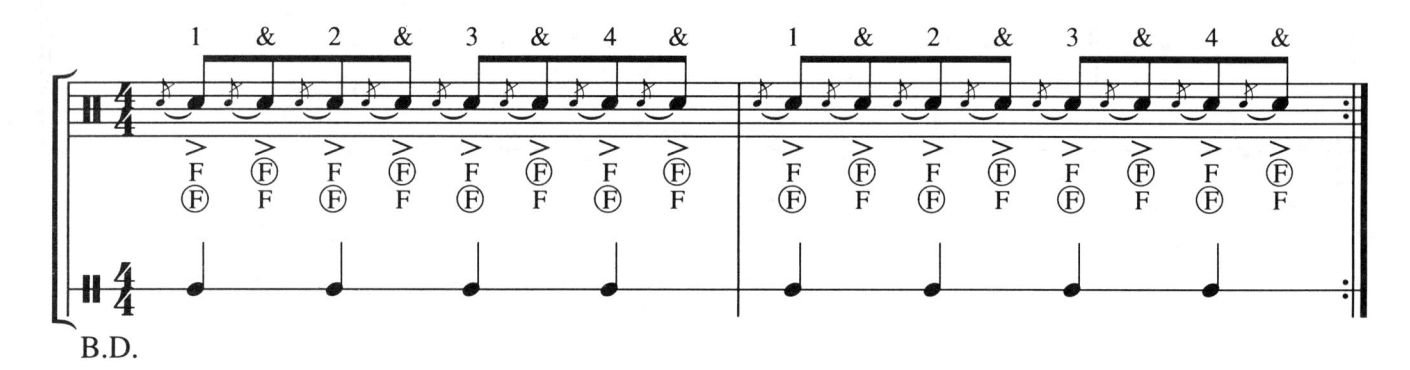

Example III

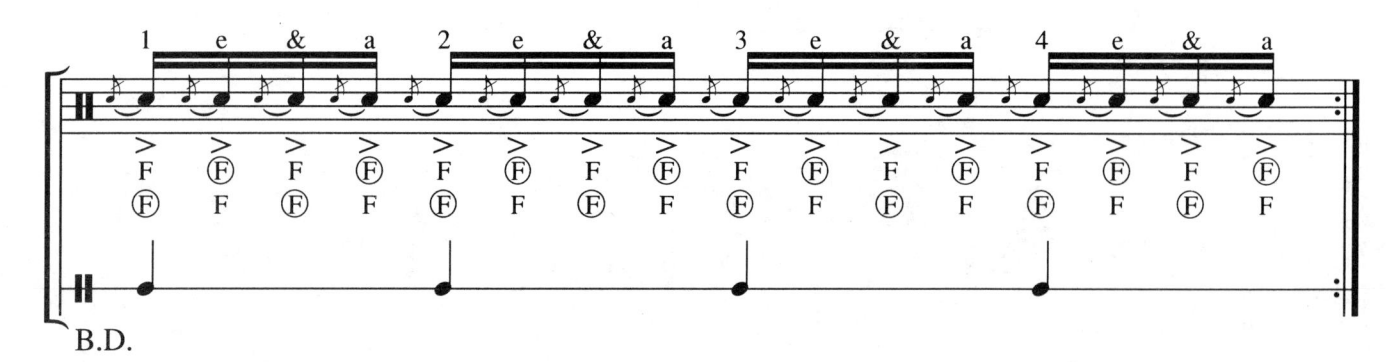

FLAM TAP

Example I

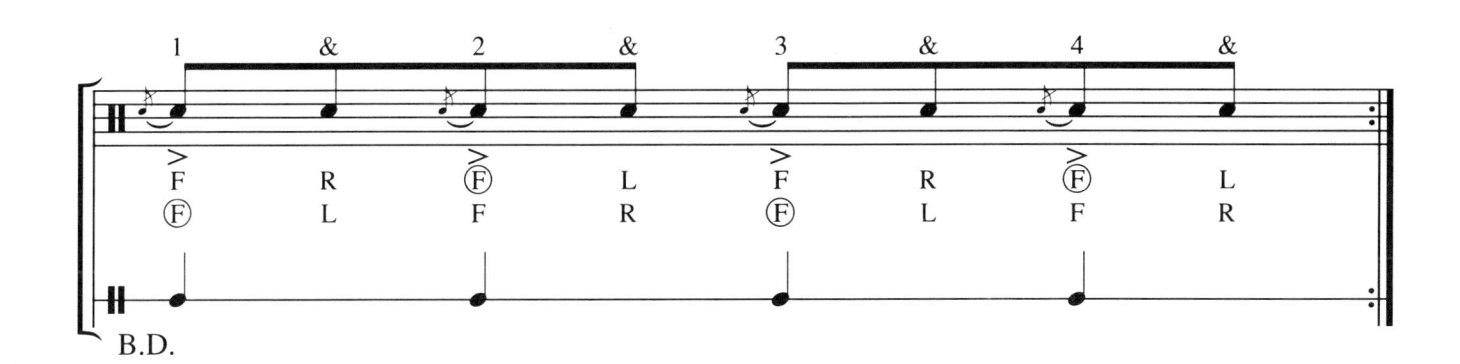

Example II

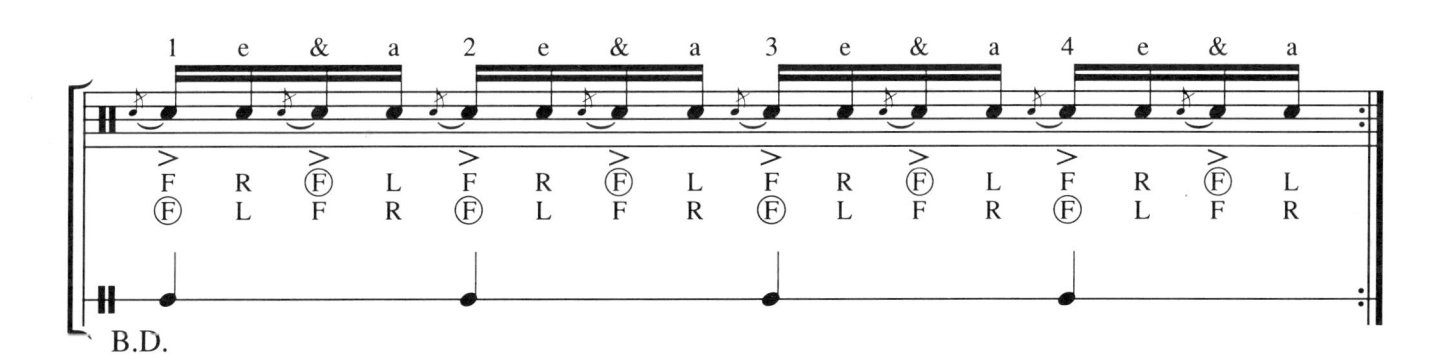

Swiss Army Triplets

Example I

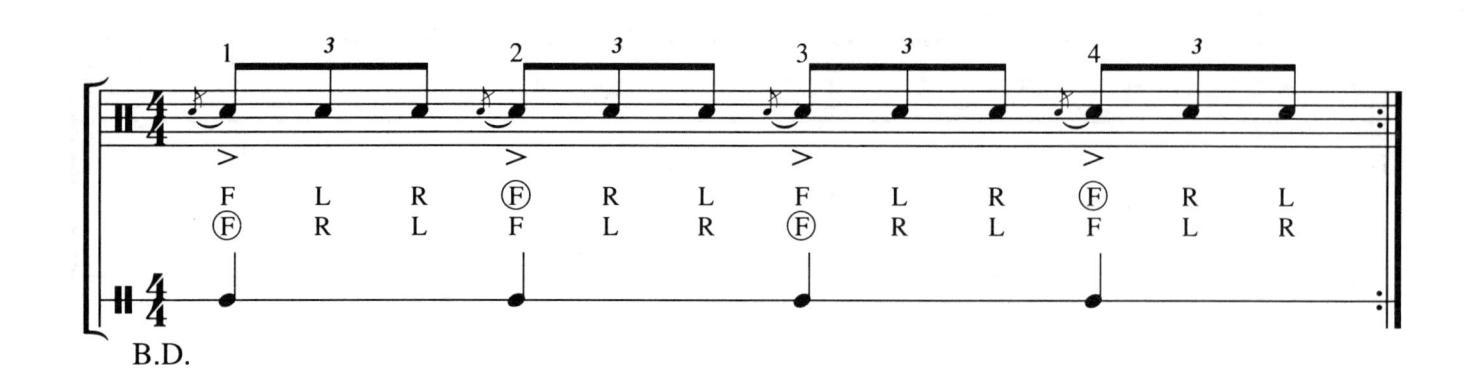

Example II

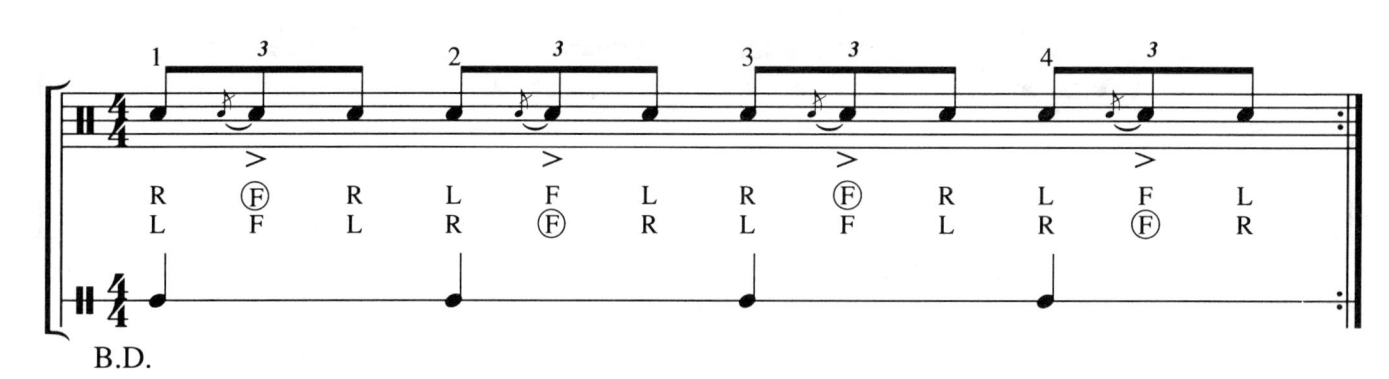

Example III

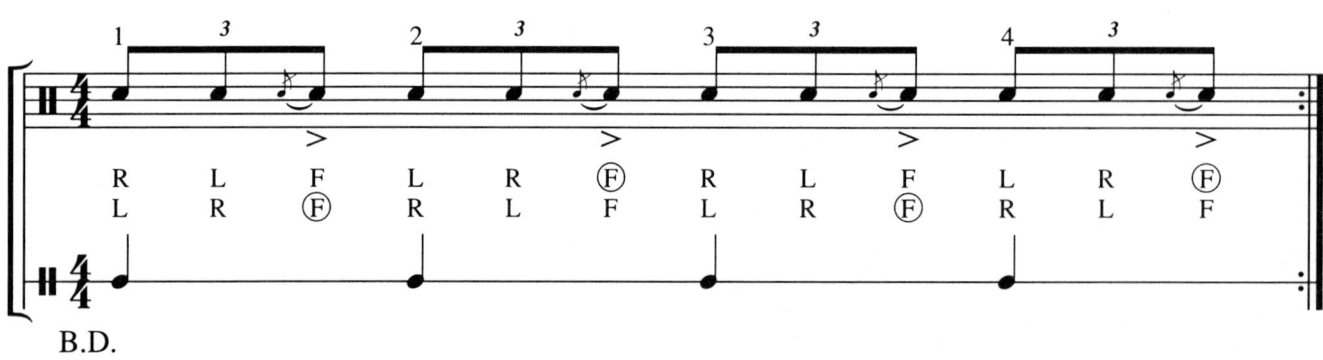

Example IV

Flam Paradiddles

Example I
Single Flam Paradiddle

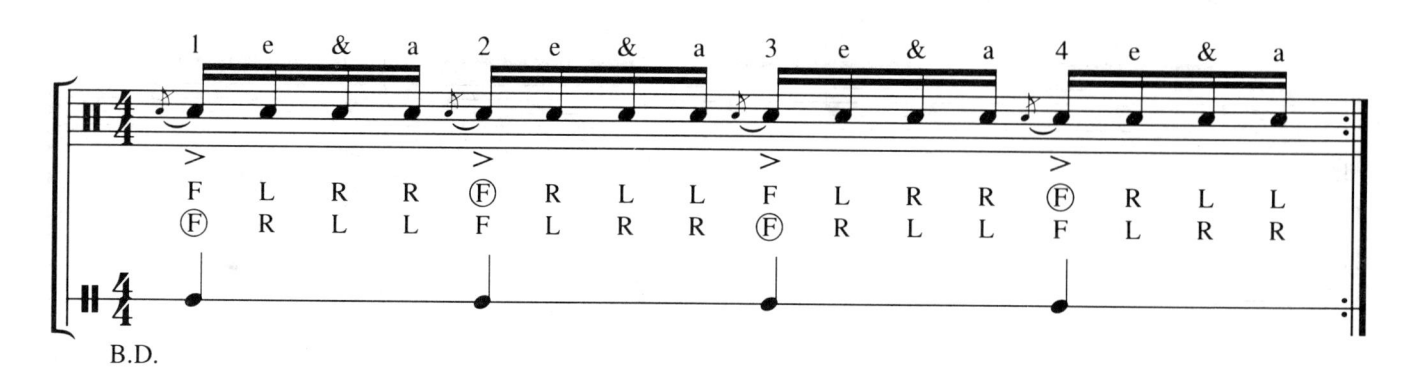

Example II (A)
Double Flam Paradiddle

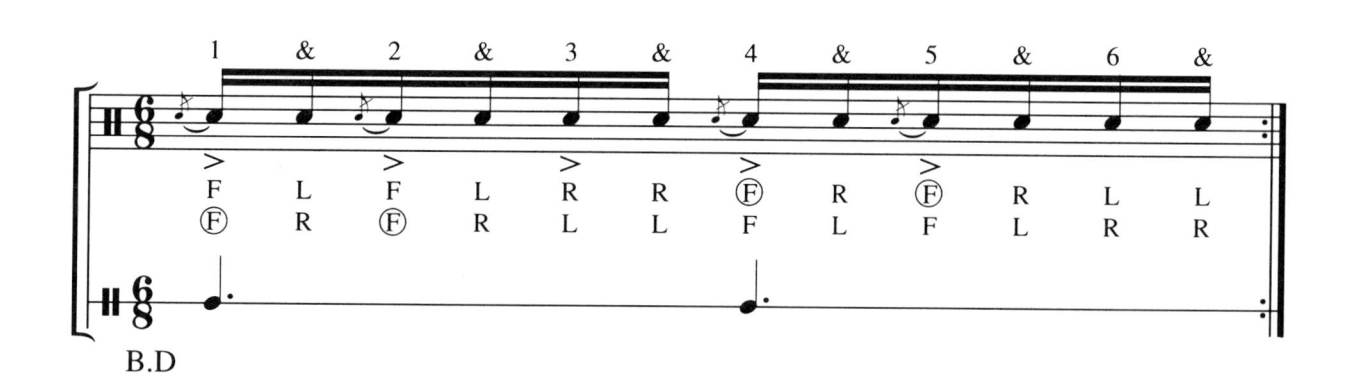

Example II (B)
Flam Double Paradiddle

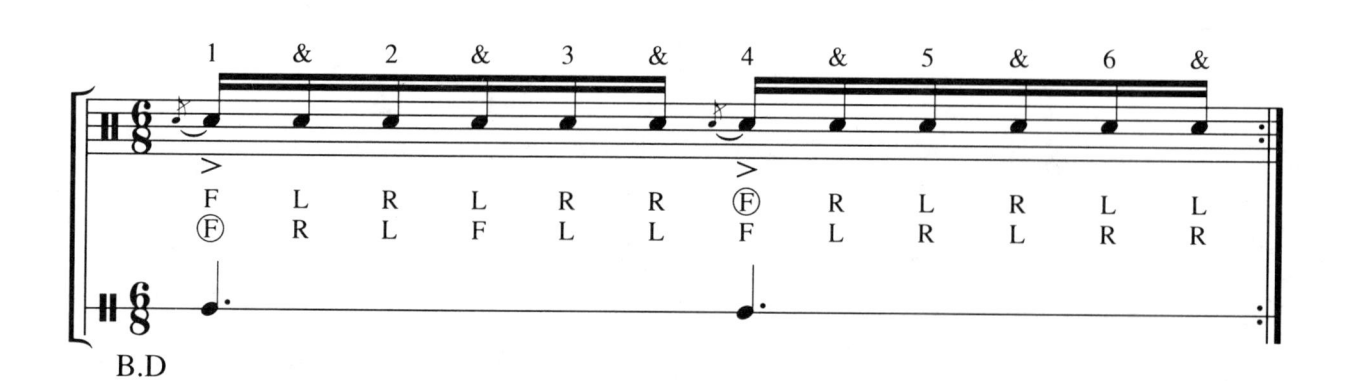

Example III (A)
Triple Flam Paradiddle

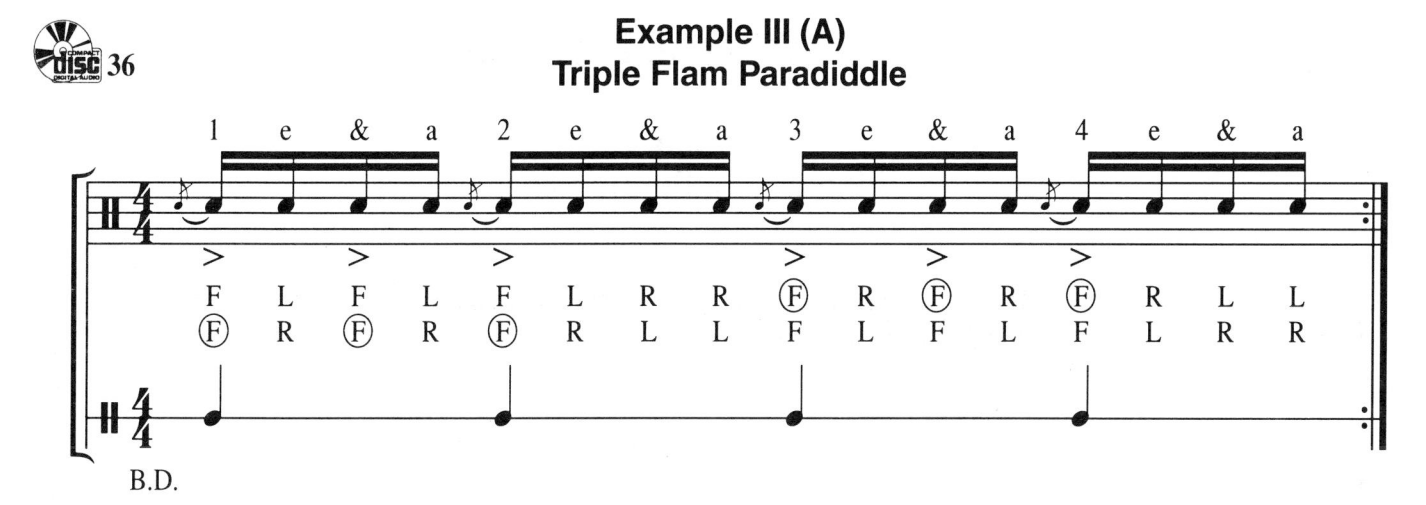

Example III (B)
Flam Triple Paradiddle

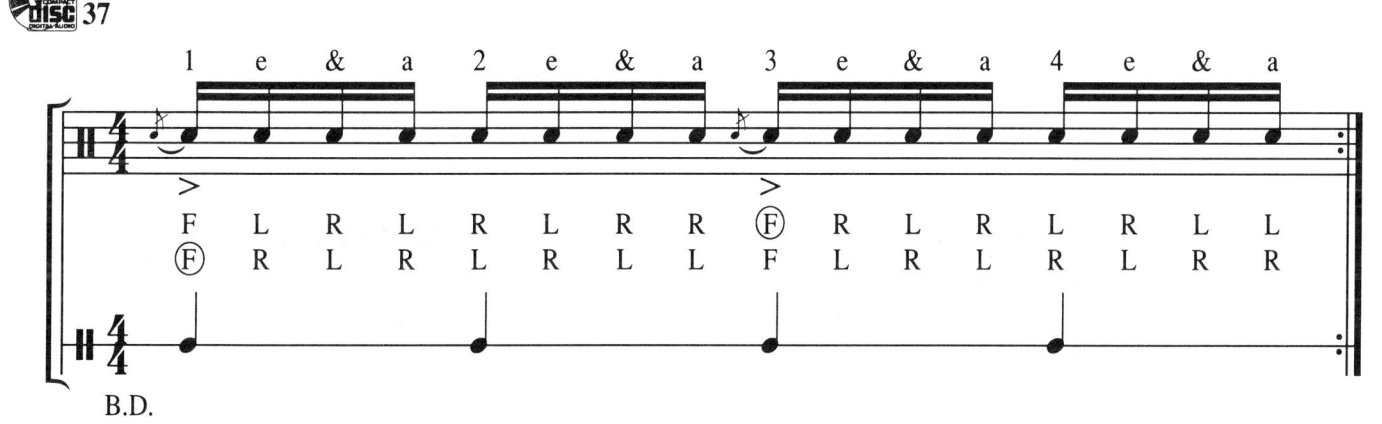

THE DRAG

The *drag* is executed by playing two grace notes with an accented primary note immediately following. The grace notes are to be bounced lightly and as close as possible to the primary note.

Example I

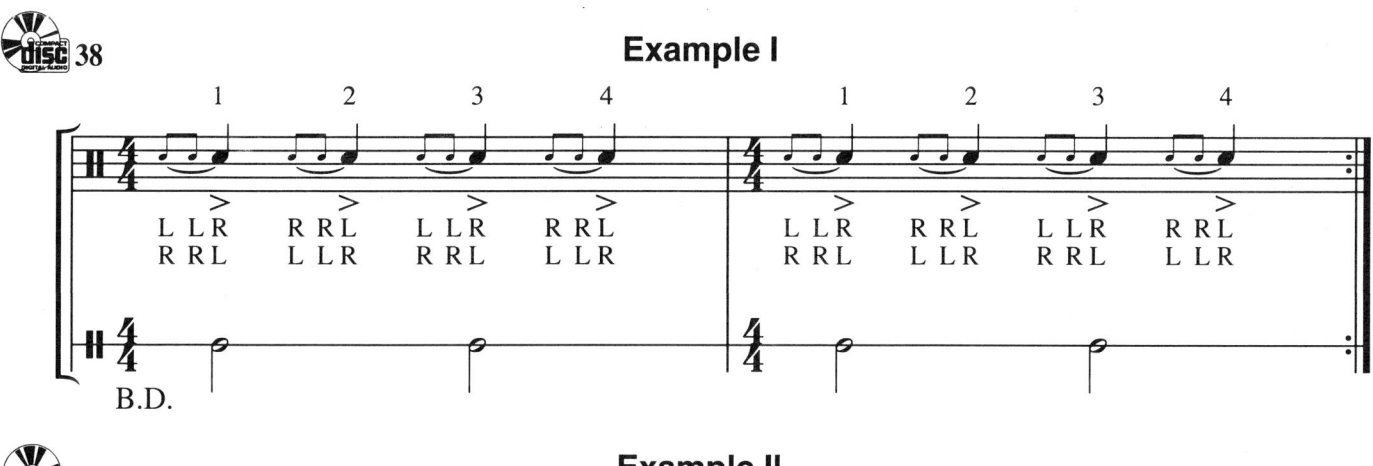

Example II

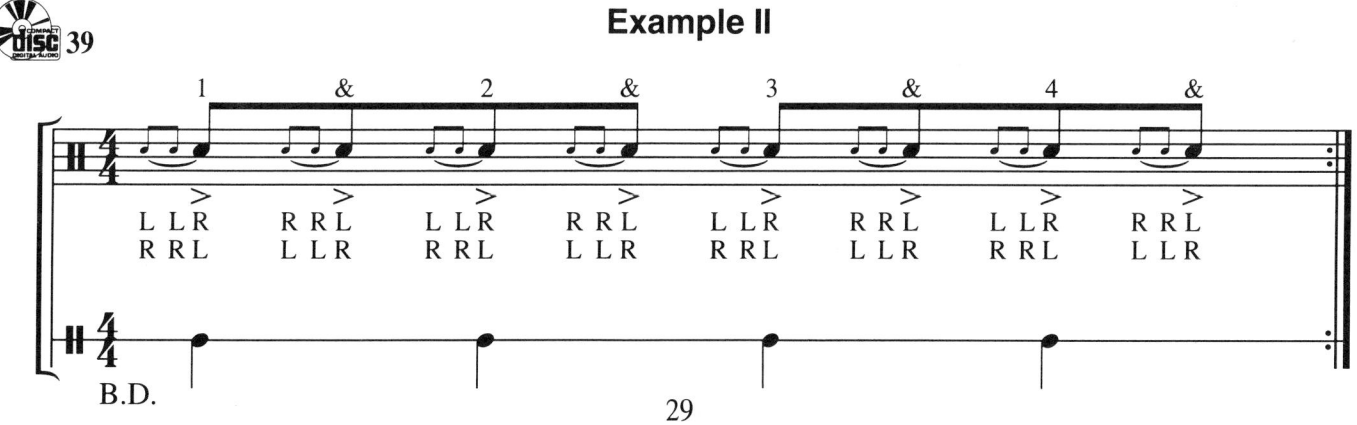

DRAG PARADIDDLES

Example I
Single Drag Paradiddle

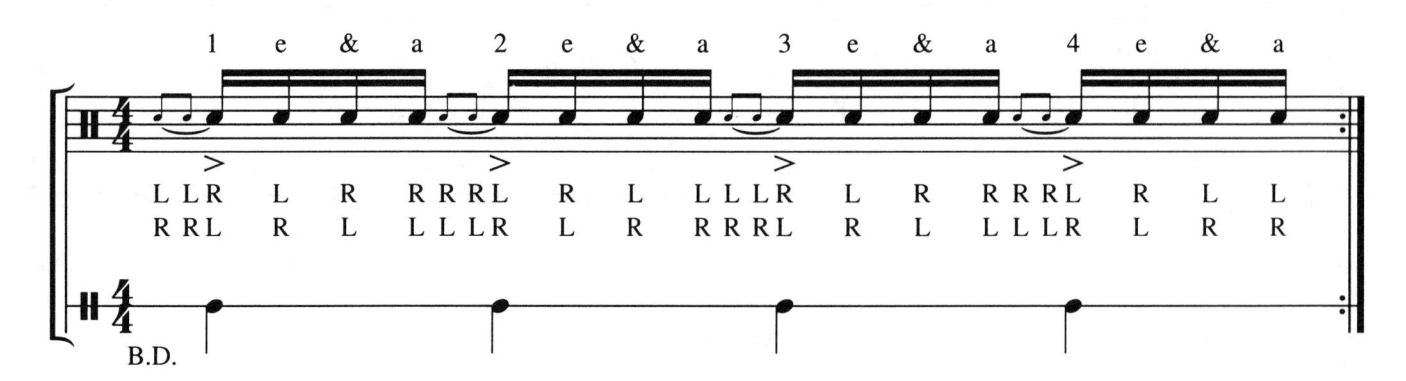

L L R L R R R L R L L L R L R R R L R L L
R R L R L L L R L R R R L R L L L R L R R

Example II (A)
Double Drag Paradiddle

L L R L L R L R R R L R R L R L L
R R L R R L R L L L R L L R L R R

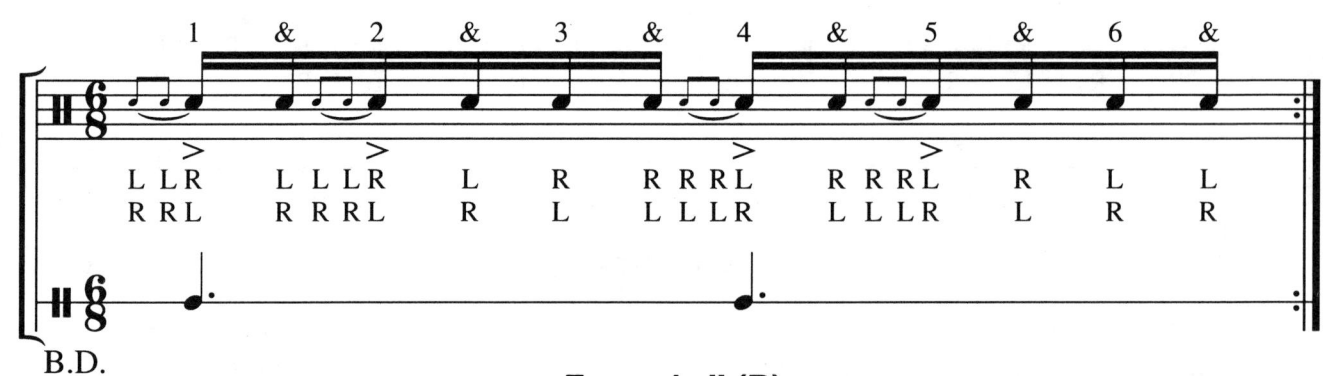

Example II (B)
Drag Double Paradiddle

L L R L R L R R R L R L R L L
R R L R L R L L L R L R L R R

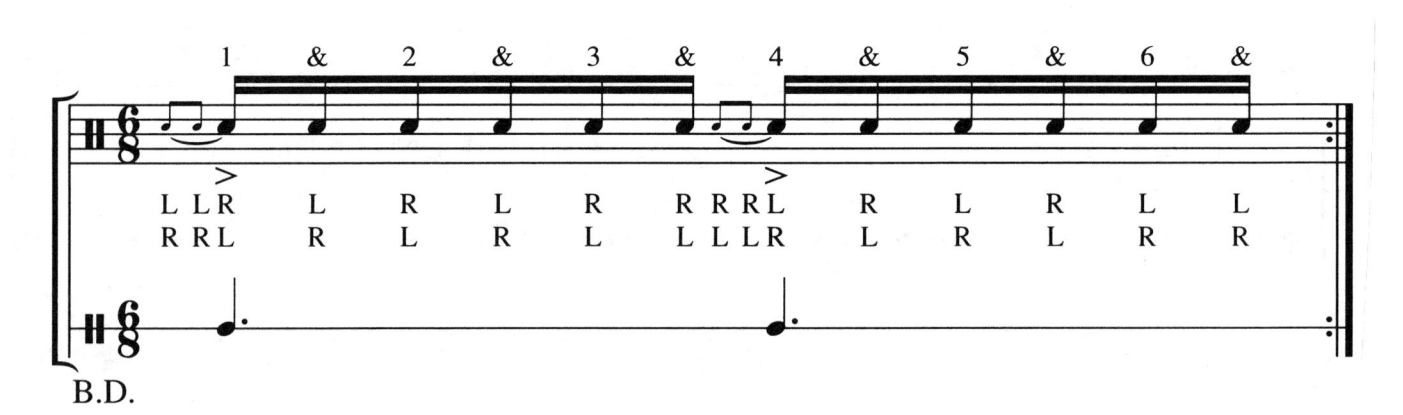

Example III (A)
Triple Drag Paradiddle

1	e	&	a	2	e	&	a	3	e	&	a	4	e	&	a
L L R	L L R	L L R	L R	R R L	R R L	R R L	R L								
R R L	R R L	R R L	R L	L L R	L L R	L L R	L R								

B.D.

Example III (B)
Drag Triple Paradiddle

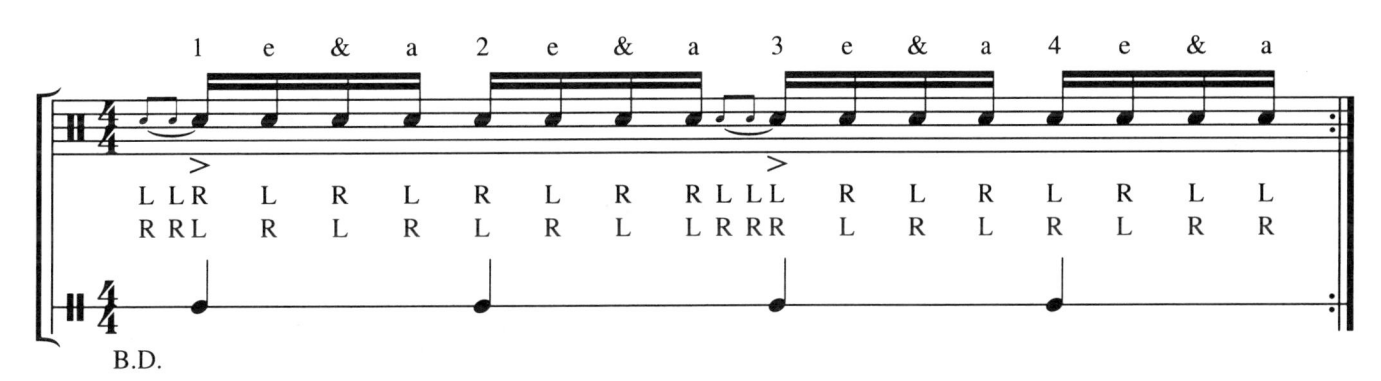

1	e	&	a	2	e	&	a	3	e	&	a	4	e	&	a
L L R	L	R	L	R	L	R	R L L	R	L	R	L	R	L	L	
R R L	R	L	R	L	R	L	L R R	L	R	L	R	L	R	R	

B.D.

THREE STROKE RUFF

This rudiment has two alternate grace notes followed by a single, accented primary note. Play the two alternate strokes as close as possible to the primary note.

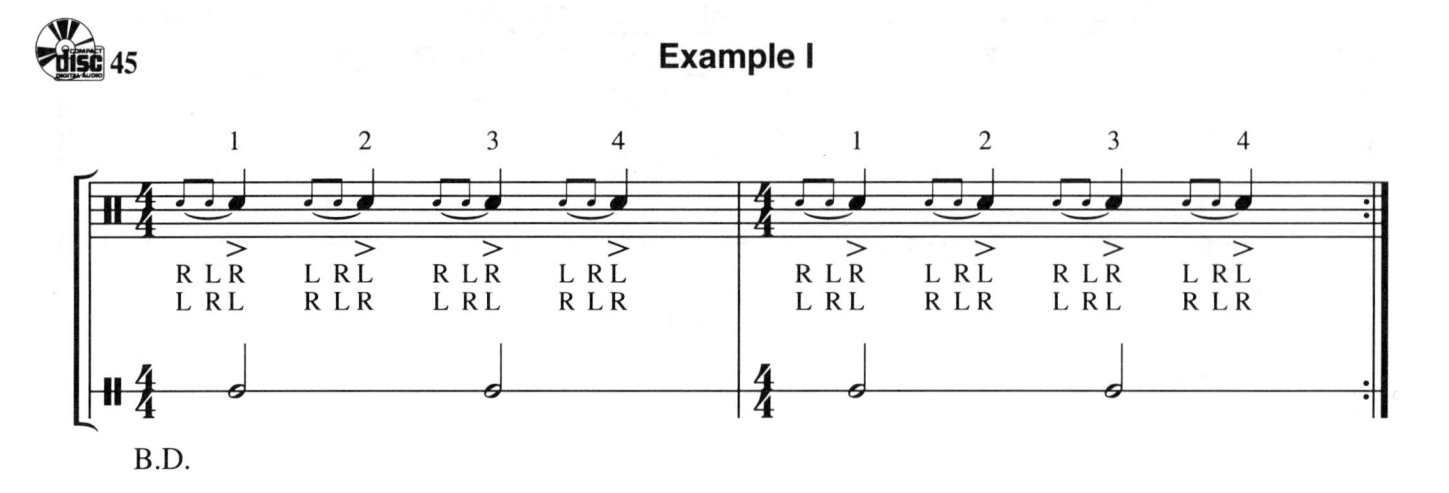

Example I

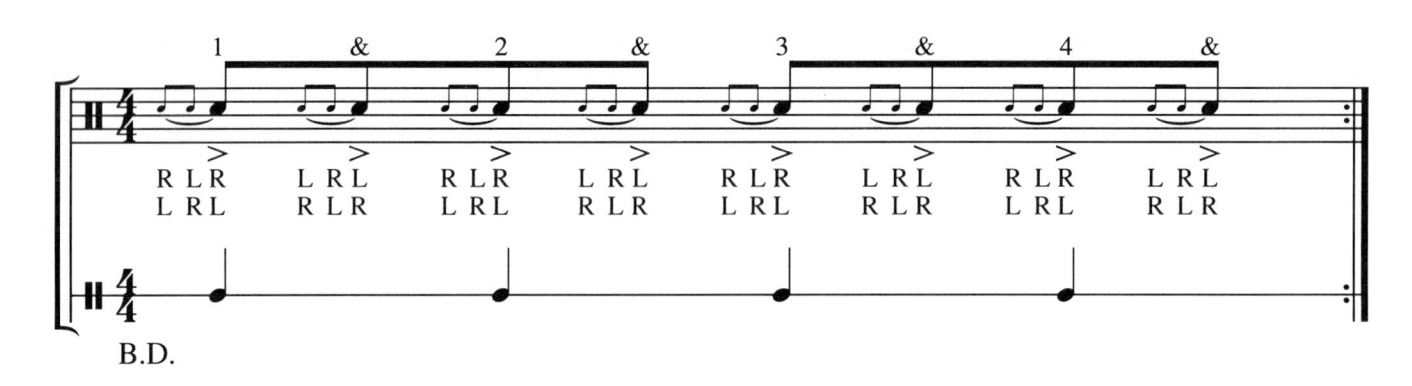

Three Stroke Ruff Paradiddles

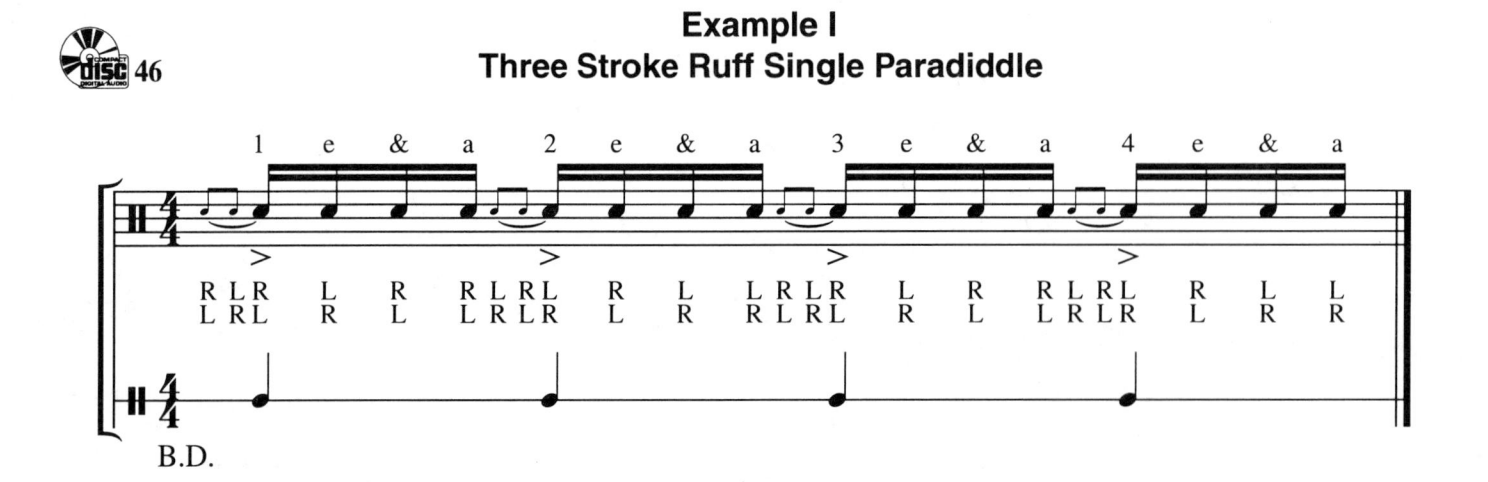

Example I
Three Stroke Ruff Single Paradiddle

Example II (A)
Three Stroke Ruff Double Paradiddle

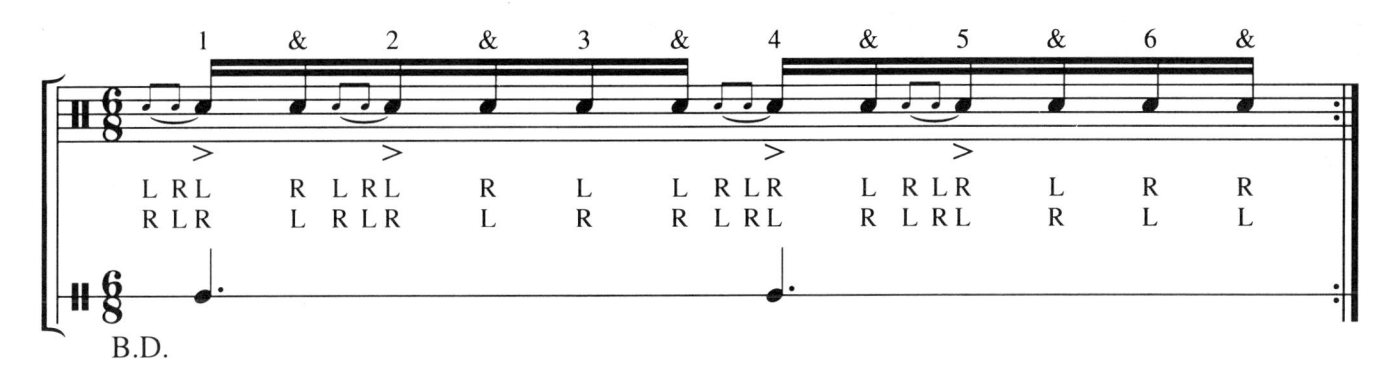

```
   1   &   2   &   3   &   4   &   5   &   6   &
   >       >               >       >
   L RL    R LRL    R   L    L RLR    L RLR    L   R   R
   R LR    L RLR    L   R    R LRL    R LRL    R   L   L
```
B.D.

Example II (B)
Three Stroke Ruff Double Paradiddle

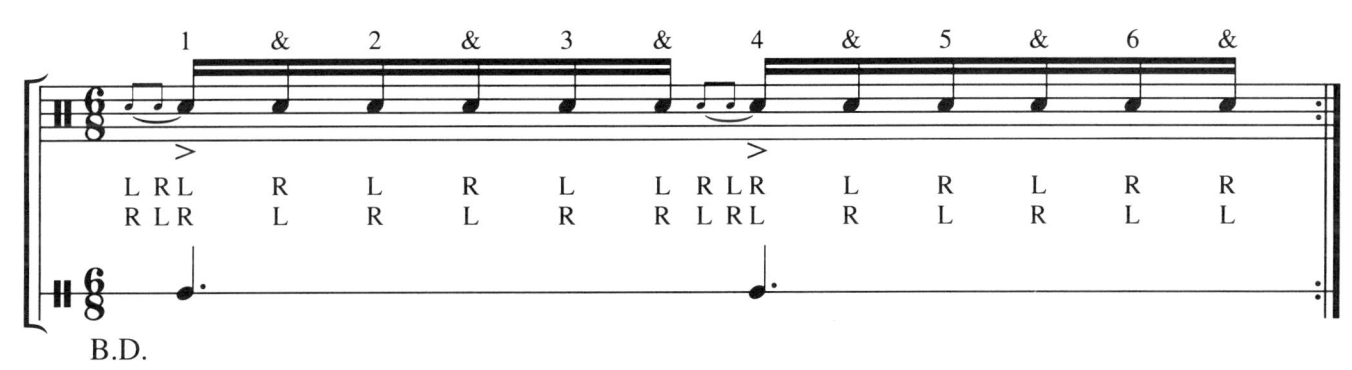

```
   1   &   2   &   3   &   4   &   5   &   6   &
   >                        >
   L RL    R    L    R   L    L RLR    L    R    L   R   R
   R LR    L    R    L   R    R LRL    R    L    R   L   L
```
B.D.

Example III (A)
Three Stroke Ruff Triple Paradiddle

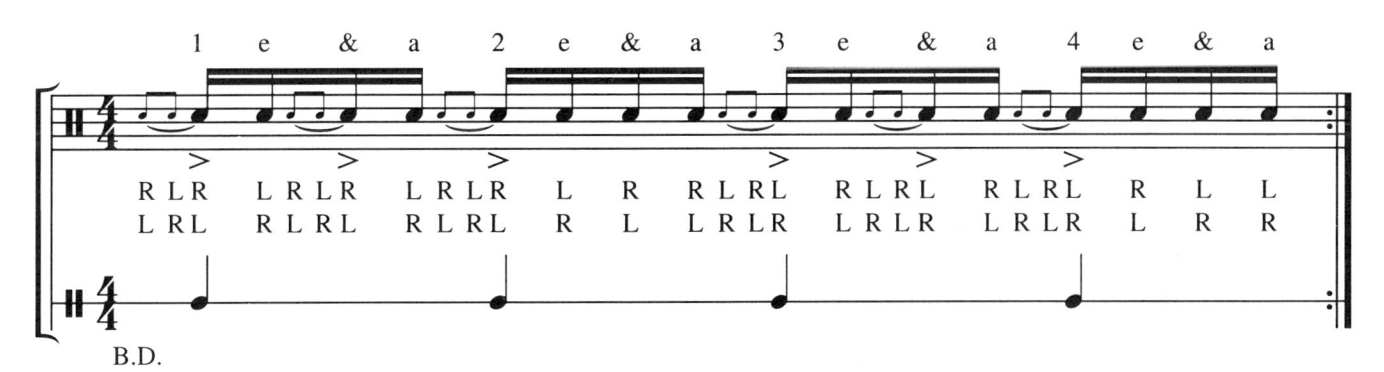

```
   1  e  &  a   2  e  &  a   3  e  &  a   4  e  &  a
   >         >         >         >         >         >
   RLR   L RLR   L RLR   L    R   RLRL   RLRL   RLRL   R  L  L
   L RL   RLRL   RLRL   R    L    LRLR   LRLR   LRLR   L  R  R
```
B.D.

Example III (B)
Three Stroke Ruff Triple Paradiddle

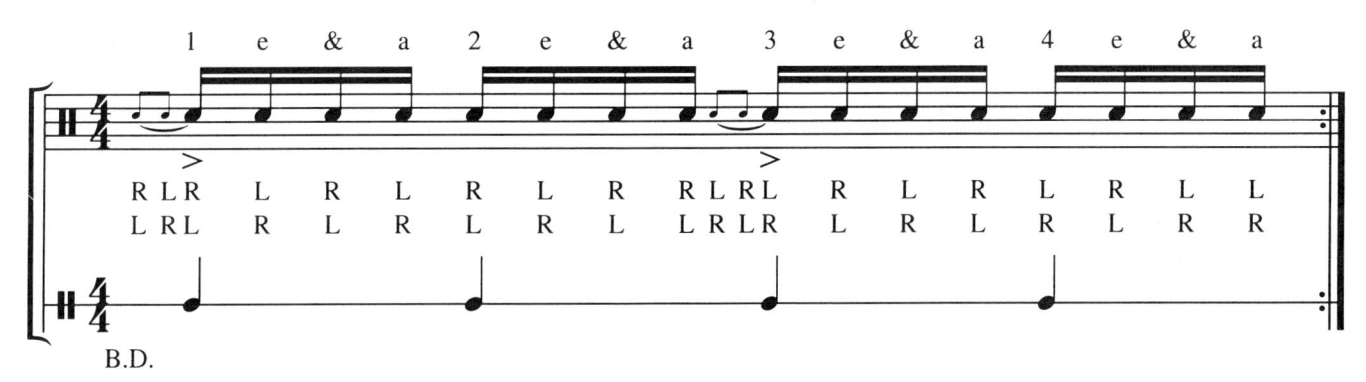

```
   1  e  &  a   2  e  &  a   3  e  &  a   4  e  &  a
   >                         >
   RLR   L   R   L   R    RLRL   R   L   R   L   R   L   L
   L RL   R    L    R    L    LRLR   L    R    L    R    L   R   R
```
B.D.

33

FOUR STROKE RUFF

The *four stroke ruff* has three alternate grace notes and one accented primary note, which is the fourth stroke. Note, if the first stroke of the rudiment is played with the left hand, then the last or fourth stroke will be played with the right hand.

Example I

```
L RLR   R LRL   L RLR   R LRL     L RLR   R LRL   L RLR   R LRL
L RLL   R LRR   L RLL   R LRR     L RLL   R LRR   L RLL   R LRR
```
B.D.

Example II

```
L RLR   R LRL   L RLR   R LRL   L RLR   R LRL   L RLR   R LRL
L RLL   R LRR   L RLL   R LRR   L RLL   R LRR   L RLL   R LRR
```
B.D.

Four Stroke Ruff Paradiddles

Example I
Four Stroke Ruff Single Paradiddle

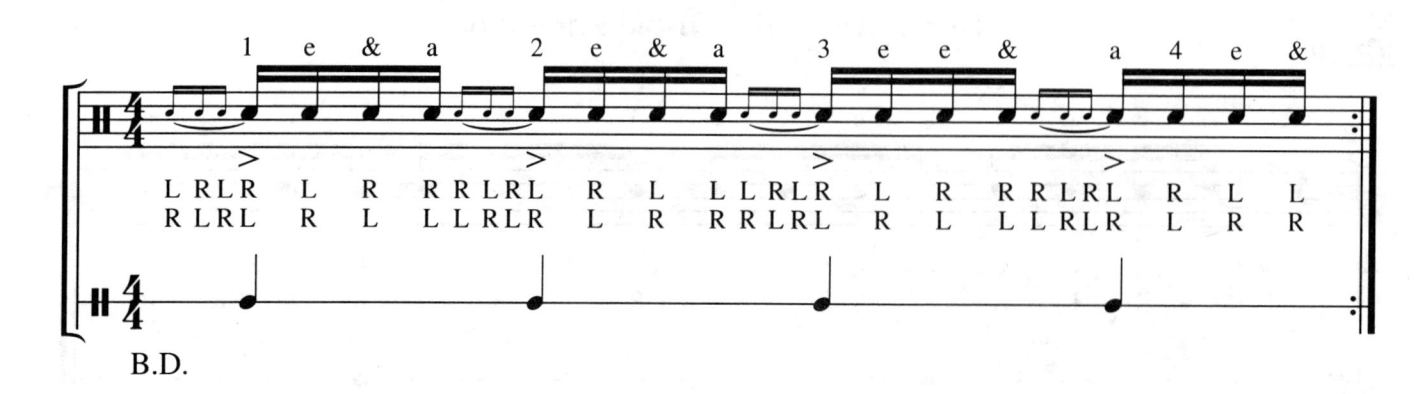

```
L RLR   L   R   R RLRL   R   L   L LRLR   L   R   R RLRL   R   L   L
R LRL   R   L   L LRLR   L   R   R RLRL   R   L   L LRLR   L   R   R
```
B.D.

Example II (A)
Four Stroke Ruff Double Paradiddle

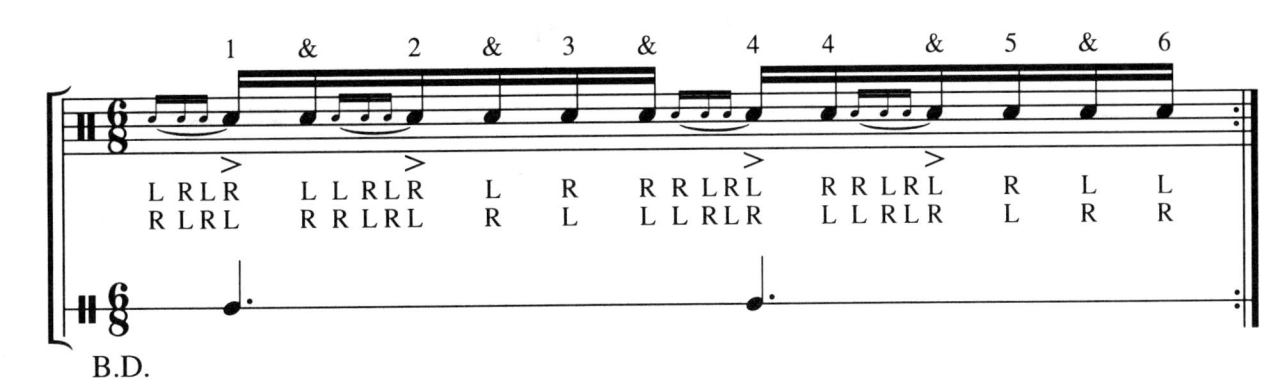

(CD 53) 6/8

L R L R   L L R L R   L   R   R R L R L   R R L R L   R   L   L
R L R L   R R L R L   R   L   L L R L R   L L R L R   L   R   R

B.D.

Example II (B)
Four Stroke Ruff Double Paradiddle

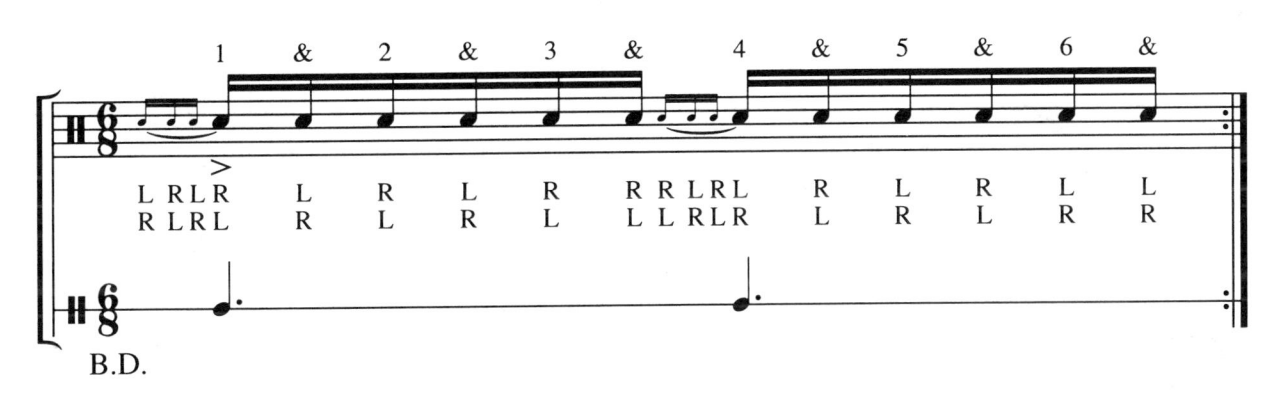

(CD 54) 6/8

L R L R   L   R   L   R   R R L R L   R   L   R   L   L
R L R L   R   L   R   L   L L R L R   L   R   L   R   R

B.D.

Example III (A)
Four Stroke Ruff Triple Paradiddle

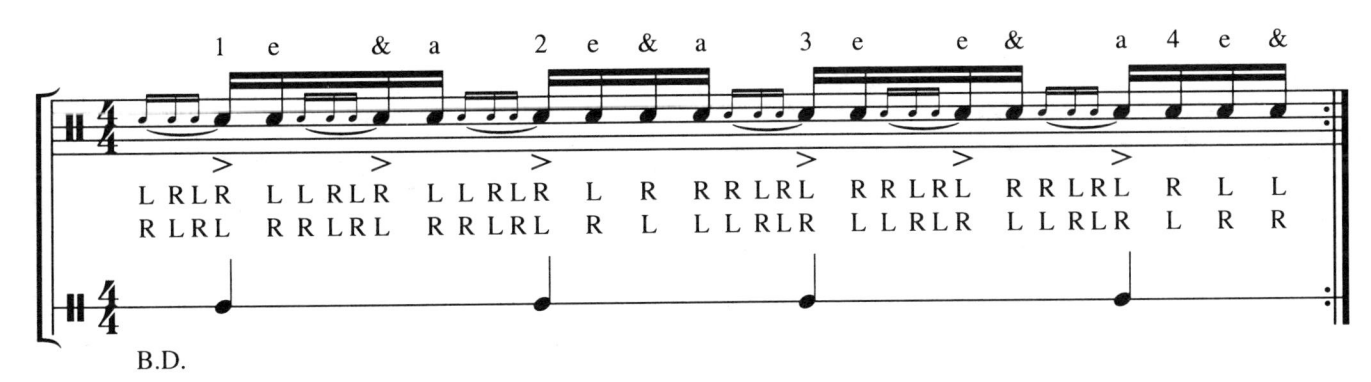

(CD 55) 4/4

L R L R   L L R L R   L L R L R   L   R   R R L R L   R R L R L   R R L R L   R   L   L
R L R L   R R L R L   R R L R L   R   L   L L R L R   L L R L R   L L R L R   L   R   R

B.D.

Example III (B)
Four Stroke Ruff Triple Paradiddle

(CD 56) 4/4

L R L R   L   R   L   R   R R L R L   R   L   R   L   L
R L R L   R   L   R   L   L L R L R   L   R   L   R   R

B.D.

PARADIDDLE-DIDDLES

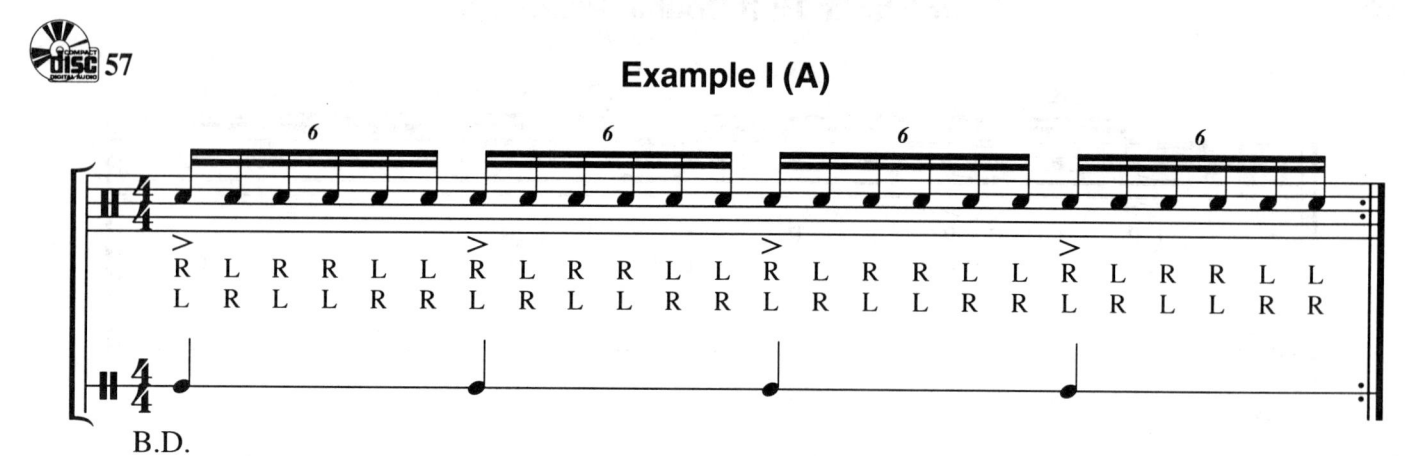

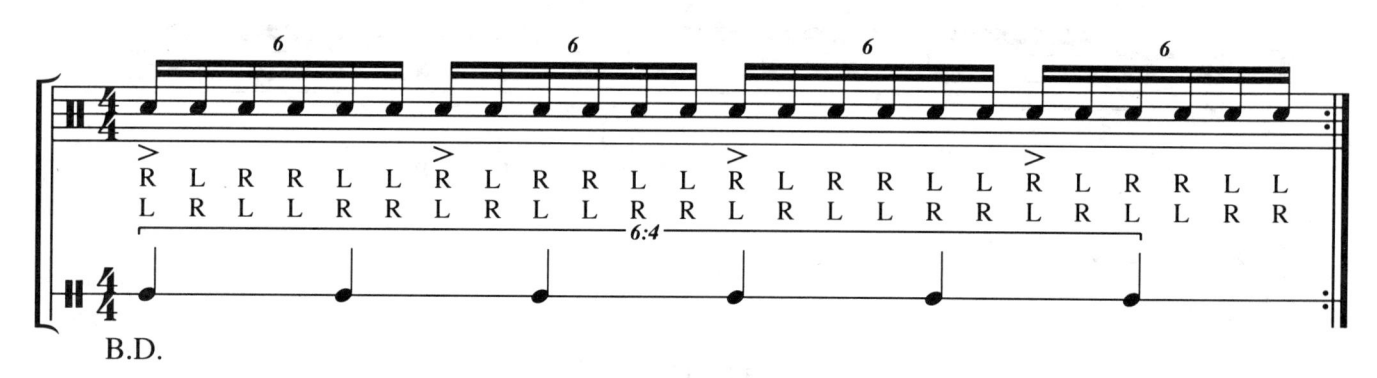

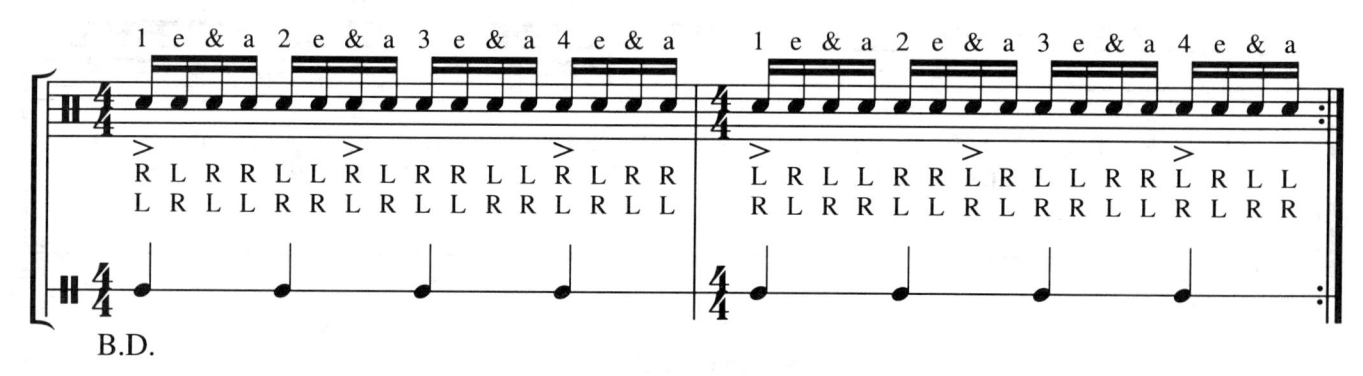

Example I (A)

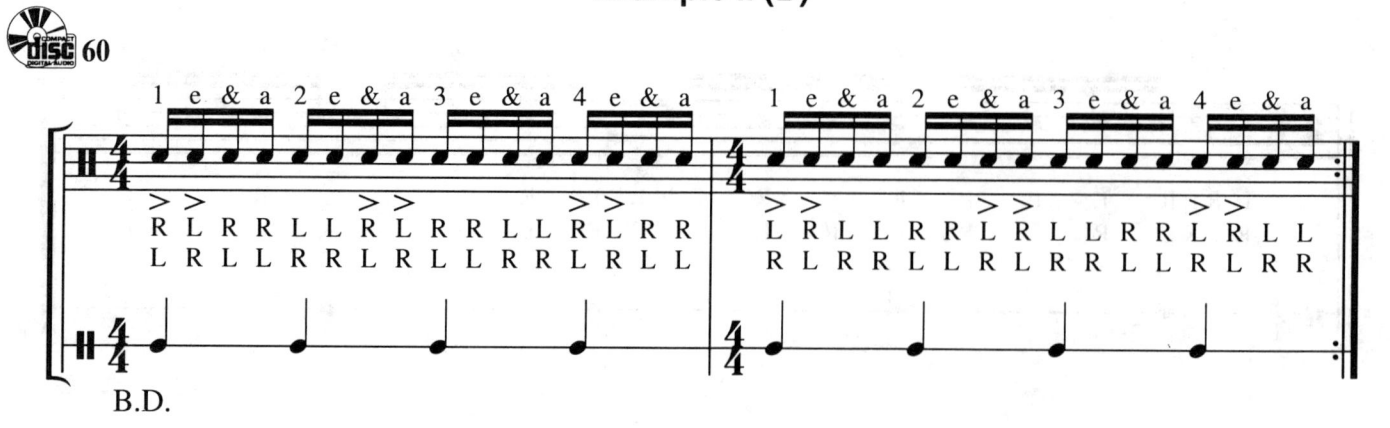

RATAMACUES

Example I (A) Single Ratamacue

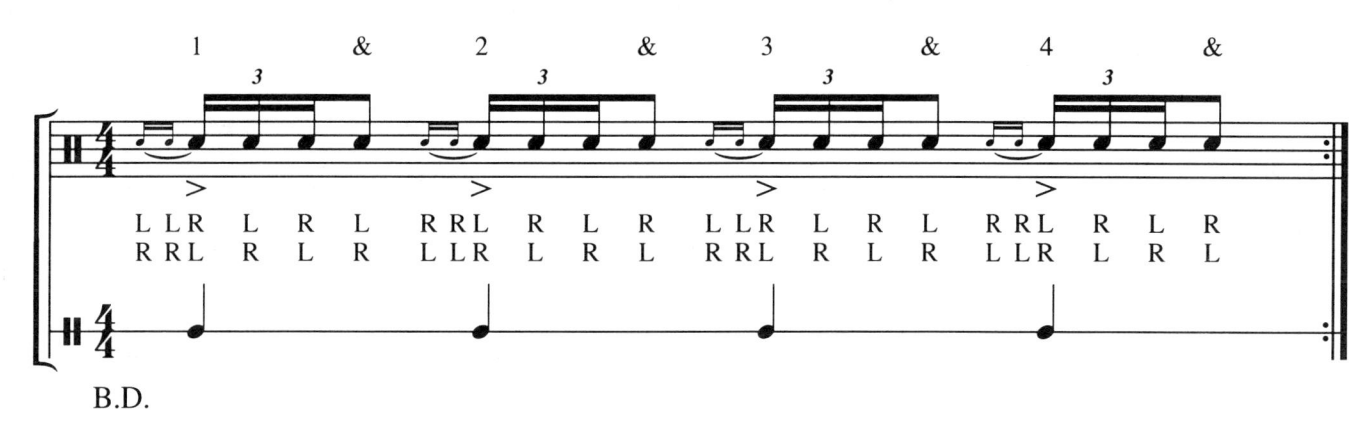

L L R L R L   R R L R L R   L L R L R L   R R L R L R
R R L R L R   L L R L R L   R R L R L R   L L R L R L

B.D.

Example I (B) Single Ratamacue (2nd inversion)

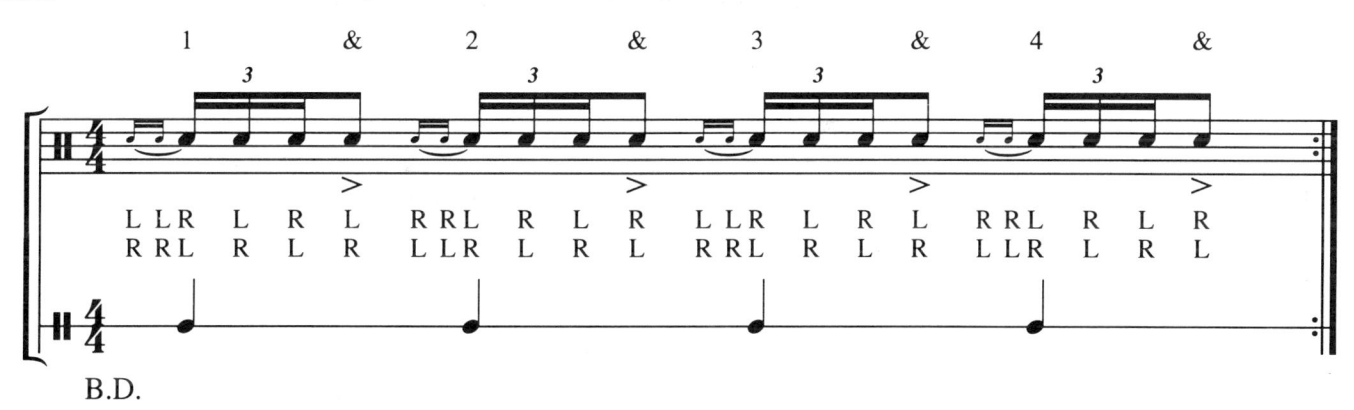

L L R L R L   R R L R L R   L L R L R L   R R L R L R
R R L R L R   L L R L R L   R R L R L R   L L R L R L

B.D.

Example II (A) Double Ratamacue

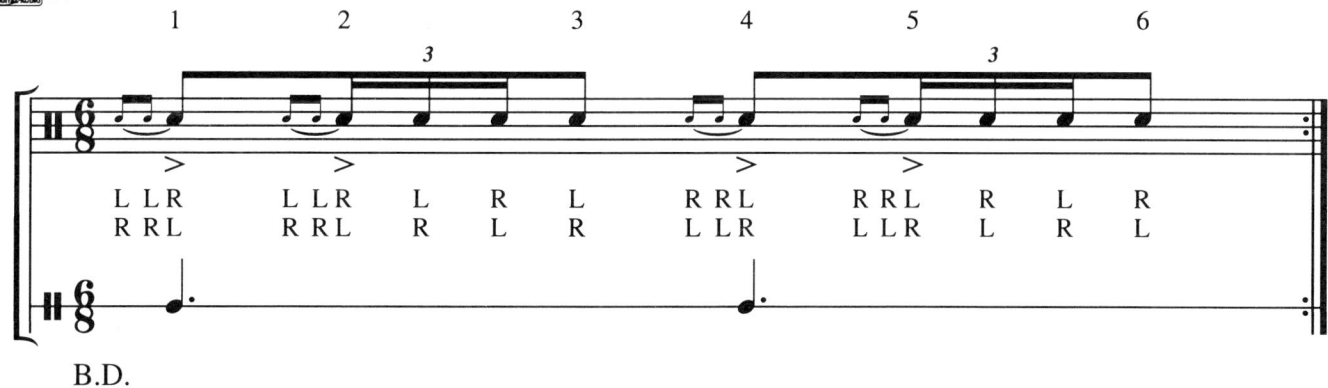

L L R   L L R   L R L   R R L   R R L   R L R
R R L   R R L   R L R   L L R   L L R   L R L

B.D.

Example II (B) Double Ratamacue (2nd inversion)

L L R   L L R   L R L   R R L   R R L   R L R
R R L   R R L   R L R   L L R   L L R   L R L

B.D.

RATAMACUES (cont.)

Example III (A) Triple Ratamacue

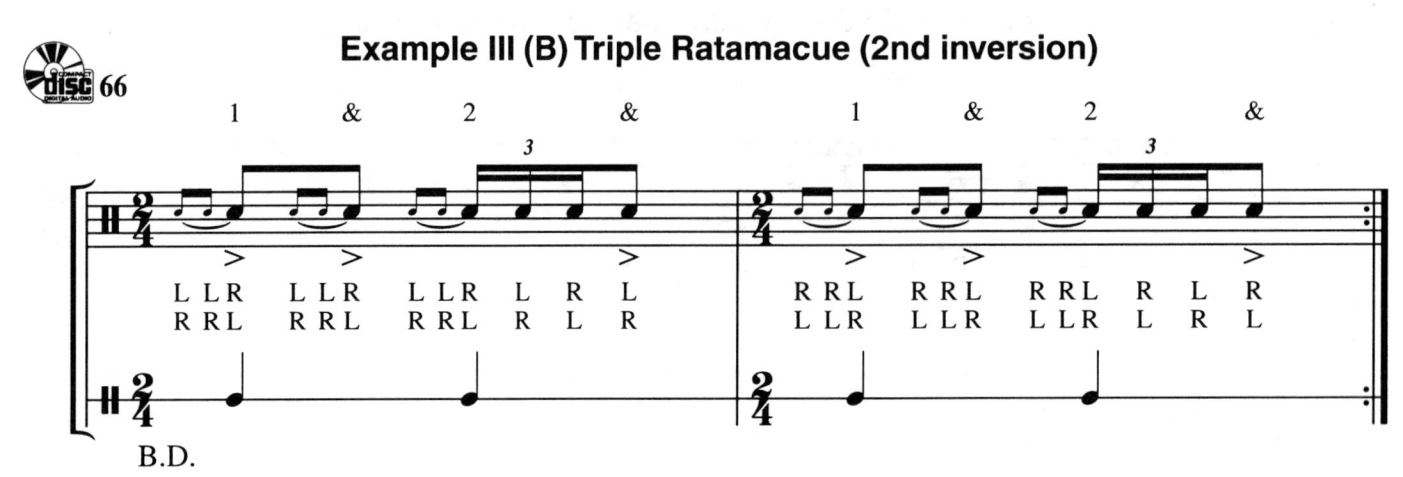

PHYSICAL ATTITUDE

Playing drums can be arduous work. In most situations you are seventy-five percent athlete and seventy-five percent musician. You seem to be giving one hundred fifty percent every night. Therefore, taking care of yourself and preventing permanent damage to your body is of great importance. Although you may think you have all the necessary means to play—i.e., staying relaxed, great technique, etc.—once you begin playing night after night you will start to feel the aches and pains of drumming. Suffering from muscle soreness is one of the few problems related to the strain of practicing/working on a regular basis. Now, let's start from the bottom of the body and move upward, and try to prevent/relieve these aches and pains.

Executing a powerful punch on the bass drum and a good kick on your hi-hat requires a specific amount of force from your legs, however, your feet will suffer the most. To alleviate the pain I recommend wearing lightweight, high-top sneakers to help support your ankles. If you must wear shoes as a job requirement they should be lightweight. Also, try buying shoes one half-size larger than you normally wear; this provides room for the placement of extra cushioning, which helps ease the discomfort caused by kicking your bass drum and hi-hat all night.

Maintaining good posture while playing for hours at a time will help keep you from developing lower back problems. Most drummers sit low with their backs rolled forward while playing. This posture leads to lower back problems. First, you will feel extremely uncomfortable and playing drums may become a real effort instead of enjoyment. Second, focusing on the back pain may cause your time to fluctuate. However, if you are already experiencing these symptoms, it is not too late to correct your posture. Find a chiropractor who can place you on an exercise program to strengthen your back. The therapy a reputable chiropractor provides may help eliminate your back problems or prevent them from occurring. **You must concentrate on keeping your back straight while playing; it will help you remain aware of what is happening musically. Keeping a straight back is the key to preventing lower back problems.**

It's a fact that repetitive hand movements may cause drummers to suffer multiple callus developments/pinched tendons, thus making it difficult to play music. Proper warming up and cooling down routines are essential in preventing these hand injuries. Work out a pre-gig practice routine for warming up and loosening up your hands. This will help you avoid injuries due to a lack of flexibility. **Also, realize that the cooling down period after a gig is just as important as the warm up!** Here are two post gig hand maintenance tips. First, ice your hands down for a few minutes immediately following the gig. Second, after taking your hands off of the ice, dry them and put a lubricating cream on them. I suggest you use a lubricating cream that contains aloe. Your hands will feel relieved and have less chance of incurring any permanent damage.

Another occupational hazard for drummers is hearing loss. Remember, when your ears ring it's because damage is occurring. A ringing in the ears is the body's warning signal that the ears are being abused. **Sometimes volume is so great it causes dizziness. This is a sign of extreme danger!** If you have experienced either of these symptoms, please see an ear specialist immediately and have them administer a hearing test. **If damage has occurred, don't dwell on it; take care of the problem immediately.** The doctor may mold a set of ear plugs to custom fit your ears. Placing a small hole in the ear plugs, to allow sound through, will enable you to play properly. It will take some adjustment time and you might not like wearing them, but in the long run earplugs may save you from developing *nerve deafness*!

We owe it to ourselves as musicians to maintain our state of well-being. We have a personal responsibility to take care of our bodies as best we can. I trust this chapter will encourage you to develop a healthy physical attitude.

MENTAL ATTITUDE

THINK POSITIVELY! BELIEVE IN YOURSELF! HAVE FAITH IN YOUR ABILITIES! Without confidence in your own skills you cannot be successful or happy. Yet, with sound self-confidence you can succeed. A sense of inferiority and inadequacy interferes with attainment in your life. Having a healthy mental attitude will bring out the creativity in your playing and help give you the happiness you need to appreciate your fellow man. Remember, as we aspire to develop into great musicians we must realize that it is also necessary to develop the inner person. Keeping a positive mental attitude is a tool for this development! **SELF-CONFIDENCE LEADS TO SELF-REALIZATION AND SUCCESS!!!**